FOUR LAST SONGS

JONATHAN STRONG

FOUR LAST SONGS

GRID BOOKS | BOSTON

ALSO BY JONATHAN STRONG

Quit the Race
The Judge's House
Hawkweed and Indian Paintbrush
More Light
Drawn from Life
Consolation
A Circle Around Her
The Old World
An Untold Tale
Offspring
Secret Words
Elsewhere
Companion Pieces:
  Doing and Undoing
  Game of Spirit
Ourselves
The Haunts of his Youth
  (*expanded from* Tike and Five Stories)

www.grid-books.org

Cover illustration by Marjorie Noyes

ISBN: 978-1-946830-06-7

FOR CARTER SNOWDEN

AUTHOR'S NOTE: I have made free prose translations of the German poems set to music by Richard Strauss in 1948. The first three are by Hermann Hesse, the last one by Joseph von Eichendorff.

I

SPRING

For a long time in shadowy depths
I dreamed of your blossoms and blue skies,
of your soft breezes and birds singing.
Now you lie here all uncovered,
bejeweled and shining before me,
wondrously drenched in light.
You know me again
and gently call to me.
All my limbs tremble
in your sweet embrace.

I DON'T WANT TO THINK ABOUT my earliest memories. I want to guess how my life went before I can remember anything at all.

What did it feel like being born? My eyelids may have felt a flash of light out there and my ears, after the rushing in the womb, may have sensed a sudden silence before I got slapped into life and let out a long wail. The army doctor would have snipped me off from my exhausted mother and tied me back into my own small self. Later he'd neatly slice away an unhygienic bit of me so I'd grow up looking like most other little American boys.

This all seems likely, but the rest I'll have to make up.

It was the steamiest day in the month of August. My father was out on early maneuvers. When they called him in he waited in muddy fatigues outside the ward until a nurse told him to go back to barracks and change clothes. My parents didn't live on base because my twenty-five-year-old dad was a married lieutenant and expecting a child, so he ran to the converted chicken barn where they lived in town and came back to the hospital in uniform, holding the stuffed rabbit he had ready for the event.

I don't think he picked me up, but he took a seat on the edge of the bed, stroked my mom's cheek, kissed her awake, and gently patted my soft head of stiff black hair. In a few weeks he would be shipping overseas.

Two years earlier when the country was just entering the war my mother had brought a still-born girl nearly to term. I might have grown up with a big sister who would've made my life different. She had been named Malinda after my mother's dead grandma. Now they named me Matthew after my father, so I was a junior like so many boys born in the war years, just in case.

When they brought me home to the chicken barn I was sleeping most of the time and suckling and messing my diapers with clear pee and mustardy slime. In consideration of his upcoming deployment my father was granted a brief leave to be with me. The bedroom had a window looking out on the ramshackle town, my own first sight of the world when I opened my blurry eyes. My dad made a pen-and-ink sketch of the view. Seventy-three years later it hangs now on the wall beside my roll-top desk. I have never been back to Louisiana where I was born.

We had those weeks together. In the cooler evenings under the reddening sky my parents took me out in the buggy they'd borrowed from my dad's army buddy's wife Barbara. I met her years later, so I know this for sure. We'd stroll through Leesville where I heard southern voices passing by. White women on our side of town exclaimed over my full head of black hair, black women smiled widely at my parents but didn't ask for a peek at me, and soldiers greeted my dad with proper salutes and hearty back slaps. I felt the bumping of the buggy along the dusty streets but wasn't old enough to smile back up at the large heads leaning over me. I only cried at stomach cramps and then settled down after a burp.

For my parents it was a dream time; for me too. But my dream seemed never-ending while theirs was overshadowed by that troop train soon to be on its way up north. There was a station platform in Alexandria where we would have the last touch of Dad's skin. He would be holding me in his arms for the last time.

When he was gone and I wasn't yet ready for travel Mom and I lived together in the converted chicken barn. My world was of bright shining days and sweaty nights, of the rubber-coated mattress and the basinette, of diapers and the nipple. I will come to that state again soon enough in my last quarter-century. I can't remember myself nestled at my mother's shoulder while she gazed out the window thinking and worrying, waiting for letters, but in the deepest squiggle of my brain there may be a fuzzy impression of the roofs and electric wires of Leesville, my first home. Or is it only Dad's pen-and-ink sketch that I see?

Barbara would come over to sit and talk and drink coffee in the mornings or have a stiff bourbon when Ron was on night duty. She'd let her little Jane crawl around on the floor and pull herself up by the bedclothes to get a glimpse of the tiny object whose soft black hair was now starting to fall out. She'd scream at my scrunched-up face and giggle when I cut a fart.

Barbara was a comfort to Mom. She knew the ropes of motherhood, but her Ron wasn't going overseas yet and she still had him at home where Mom had only me. They liked to talk and drink together late into the evenings after Jane had curled up on her mother's lap at the kitchen table and I was freshly diapered and asleep in Jane's borrowed crib. Mom sipped slowly, but Barbara would knock a few back and get rowdy. "We need this," she'd say. "How are ordinary gals like us supposed to get through all this shittiness?" She let out her anxieties, but my mother kept hers to herself. She'd laugh at her friend's rants and didn't mind when Barbara got sloppy by eleven o'clock and needed a dishrag to wipe her eyes. All the time Mom was thinking, "But your husband's not gone over yet and I've only had two letters, one from New Orleans that doesn't count and one from when he passed through D.C. sounding fretful about me and little Matthew but not much about the boat waiting for him in New York City.

Still Barbara's visits helped. The loudmouth friend was a fun distraction. I don't know if I was a comfort or a complication. I kept Mom busy when I was awake, and when I slept I let her sleep longer than she was used to. She adopted my rhythm, but while I was peaceful and contented she was depressed and lonely. What could nine or ten pounds of a digesting operation do to soothe a young wife whose husband had gone to war? But Malinda had never actually been there and now I was.

When at last the army doctor said I'd be fine to make the trip Mom and I got ready to leave my native state. Another couple from Camp Polk was eager to take our floor of the chicken barn. Barbara got back her crib and buggy and helped us pack. My part was easy: the rubber basinette held my flannel blankets and snap-up terrycloth suits and my rabbit. They filled the bottom layer of Mom's steamer trunk. All I needed on the train were my diapers and my mother's breast. I knew nothing about the war or my father on his way to it.

Ron had the use of an officer's car and drove us, Barbara clinging onto Mom the whole way, to the same station in Alexandria where my father had made his farewell. We were heading straight north to a Chicago suburb for his mother to take us in because Mom's own parents were separated and neither had extra room.

The train sounds felt like being back in the womb, all that rushing and chugging and jostling, or like a long buggy ride around Leesville with cars rumbling by and horns honking. I had no sense of beginnings or ends. Other passengers stopped to admire the sleeping baby, and the porter made much of me while he set up the compartment each night. He'd talk close by my little ears in his deep southern voice. I wouldn't regularly be hearing men's voices for some time to come.

When the choo-chooing came to a halt with a final great blast of steam I was carried out into a loud city and then into the back seat of Aunt Alicia's blue 1940 Oldsmobile. There is a faded photo of us arriving in Grandmother Heath's driveway. Here was a nearly silent world of tall green trees and flowers and soft lawns, and I may have felt its strangeness after my dusty first home. The early fall air was cool with a pleasant breeze. The pale yellow frame bungalow had only one story, no more rickety stairs for Mom to lug me up to a stuffy set of rooms under a barn roof.

Mom and Grandmother didn't talk much. Each had her own thoughts set on the absent Matthew. They did read each other the first letters he'd sent them and waited hopefully every day for the mail. Mom and I got the guest room next to Grandmother's, so I had to keep extra quiet in the mornings not to wake her. Dad's older brother John was stationed somewhere in the Pacific and Aunt Alicia had their two kids with her down the hall in the brothers' old room, my aunt in my uncle's bed and Sally and Richie in my dad's. Those two would stampede around disturbing Grandmother's peace and their mother did little to control them. Mom felt herself the preferred daughter-in-law.

When she took me to my other grandmother's apartment above the dry goods store in the village I was quickly jiggled into silence if I cried because they had more on their minds, not just my dad but my grandparents' pending divorce. I wasn't allowed to see Mom's dad who lived in the city. She was expected to take sides in the domestic battle, which Mom later joked sometimes seemed as dire as the war.

Grandmother Heath, in sacrifice to the war effort, had given up her peaceful solitary widowhood of gardening and playing her record albums on the Capehart automatic changer. She now had a houseful. She wished Alicia might soon be evacuating herself and kids back to Rock Island, but that daughter-in-law had taken to the easy suburban life and didn't actually miss her own parents. Instead she had assigned herself the task of enlivening the lonesome widow's days: nothing like the patter of tiny feet to bring joy to an old lady, who was in truth only fifty-five.

My feet didn't patter yet. I kept doing the things I did best, swallowing food and ejecting what I hadn't managed to convert into burgeoning flesh. My eyes twinkled whenever Grandmother cooed at me or a bird perched on the feeder out the kitchen window, but they would squint in anger at cousin Richie's over-strenuous hugs and cousin Sally's pokes and prods. "They love baby Matthew so much!" Aunt Alicia would say. "It's educational, learning to care for someone smaller than yourself."

Despite them I did feel cared for. Grandfather Heath had once built a wooden cradle on rockers for his boys where I now lay bundled up with Grandmother's foot gently tapping me to and fro while Mom was out shopping. Before supper we would all gather in the living room to hear war news on the radio, the one time my aunt shushed up her little devils. Letters did come, and I heard them read aloud but understood nothing except perhaps the happy rise or solemn fall of women's voices. The assault on Germany was underway with my father somewhere in the midst of it. My cousins gleaned some notion of this, but what could I absorb from the gobbledegook of "Your brave Uncle Matthew is marching across France, kiddos! And your daddy's on that faraway island fixing up airplanes. Isn't that neat!" I was sleeping blissfully through the last months of the Second World War.

Grandmother was quite a smoker. Aunt Alicia had to go around wiping out the heavy glass ashtrays so her two devils wouldn't make more mess. My mom ramped up her own smoking habit, Camels instead of Grandmother's Chesterfields not to mix up their packs. Sometimes Grandmother would bring out her Brownie camera and snap at us grandkids. I still have the album of hazy off-center black-and-whites and occasional color ones of special events like Sally blowing out her third-birthday-cake candles. After tearing open her presents she went dancing wildly around the room until she fell and cut her lip on the hearthstone. It bled all over the red oriental rug. Years later, still living in that house, I noticed the dull brown stain that blended with the pattern and Grandmother told me how it got there. "It's Sally's earliest memory," she said, "blood gushing out her mouth while she screamed blue murder." Somewhere around turning three, I guess, is the beginning of memorable life. When I was only six months old I had a long wait ahead of me.

Winter had set in and then the new year and fewer letters came from Europe though Aunt Alicia heard regularly from Uncle John. The newspaper allowed Mom to follow the general locations of Dad's unit, but it was a fearful time. For Christmas Aunt Alicia had taken her kids to Rock Island and Grandmother confided in Mom that she hoped they might stay, but they didn't. Mom claimed she liked having them around, which wasn't true, but those rambunctious cousins did cast me in a good light. I was a docile baby even when I began to nudge myself along the floorboards in my knit pajamas. I had become quite attached to my rabbit and wanted it beside me all the time. If Richie grabbed it and ran off I would let out a furious scream, not my usual piteous whimper for attention or solace. My aunt would snatch the rabbit out of Richie's tight smudgy grasp and then he would be the screamer while I placidly squeezed my best pal close and forgot it had ever been gone.

Professors say we must develop a sense of object constancy to secure our own places in the world. I had certainly adjusted to my mother's comings and goings or my grandmother leaving a smoking butt in an ashtray when she went to check on dinner cooking. I clearly didn't mind when my cousins left me alone and somehow I knew not to expect much from Aunt Alicia, but I had to have that rabbit.

I don't know when I determined it was a he. The sounds I was beginning to make made no sense though Mom insisted she could interpret them. She'd hold up my companion and say "Rabbit?" and I'd reach out more for the thing than the word. At some point if he was left in the other room and she said "Rabbit?" I might have made the connection the way my dog does when I say "Walk?" But I have no idea how or when words began to mean things. By February I could say "Momma" and "Gomma," and "Tonna" for Aunt Alicia, among the few landmarks Mom noted in my baby book, which is otherwise largely empty after the page with my newborn statistics. I imagine my mother was rather depressed those months and terribly anxious. Smoking and a little drinking helped, but between dealing with me, worrying about Dad, negotiating with her sister-in-law, and dutifully supplying Grandmother's needs Mom had no time to find a new Barbara to pal around with though they did talk long distance once in a while and corresponded with less and less to say to each other.

There was one other new baby down the block, and sometimes Mom met up with Mrs. Templeton at the corner park and set me in the sandbox with a drooling little crawler named Beau. I doubt we had much to do with each other then. I probably stared at him wondering how there could be another being my size. I'd only known kids who could run and dance and babble and large women who fed me, cleaned me, and rocked me to sleep.

When my teeth were coming in Mom would rub a finger of bourbon over my gums to stop my squalling. I had such pure emotions in those days. It may come to that at the end when all I'll know is pain and hunger and fear but also relief. Back then I'd smile or chortle or fall instantly asleep on Mom's shoulder and may have mitigated her depression, but she could no longer take comfort from our moments together after she'd learned of my father's death in the war.

She was out shopping for groceries when Grandmother opened the front door to two uniformed men and knew immediately what had happened. It couldn't be her first son John, who was safe in Hawaii. It had to be Matthew in France. Aunt Alicia, tiptoeing in from three napping children, saw Grandmother's hands fluttering in the air and rushed to catch her before she fell. From the soldiers she took some papers and a folded flag, murmured her thanks, and reached for the doorknob to shut out the messengers standing helplessly on the cold front step in the early morning light.

Then Mom had driven home in the blue Oldsmobile and came in the back door with a paper sack in each arm. She set them on the kitchen counter and began putting things away in their proper places then wondered at the silence. Looking into the living room she saw Alicia's arm around the bent shoulders of the mother who'd lost her younger son. They were side by side on the couch where they never sat together. Mom caught sight of the blue cloth of white stars on the coffee table.

But soon it was spring with the dark winter lifting itself afar. The war in Europe would end in a matter of weeks. Now every year when the trees start to bud and the crabapple tree out my study window blossoms pink and white I think of things I seldom think about the rest of the year. Back then I was the only creature in the house with no thought of death. Even the cousins, three and nearly two, had a faint notion that their uncle would never come home again. I wonder if Mom was angry at me for not knowing.

In spring my world was expanding. I smelled new smells and gazed up at greening trees while Mom pushed me down the shady sidewalk in Richie's outgrown stroller. I heard the birds and felt the sun and my limbs seemed part of the whole me. I began to know I was Matthew, and in the sandbox I now knew Beau by the sound of his name. We'd chuckle at each other and fuss over a rubber dump truck rumbling along in the sand. Mrs. Templeton was now Cathy and my mom was Julie when they talked to each other always in low voices, never raucous like Barbara, whose last letter was somewhat tear-stained on my dad's account, though Ron was coming home to her as Mr. Templeton was to Cathy.

My dad's ashes were in an urn they placed in the stone wall of Grandmother's Episcopal churchyard. I was there, held in Mom's arms. Grandmother only went to church for christenings, marriages, and funerals, and when I was old enough I'd accompany her but we never stopped at the wall with her husband's brass plate next to her son's. Her own went up nearly half a century ago now, which was when I finally saw all three of them together.

Uncle John did come home safe. He bought a house for his family in the next village and took a job with an electrical appliance firm, so I lived on in a quieter house with two women who mostly went their own ways in subdued sadness. Grandmother worked in her garden with her eye shade and knee pads and after supper put on her heavy breakable seventy-eights of symphonies and opera arias. I heard the music, terrified as I was of Rachmaninoff's greenish face on an album cover. Outside I'd smile at the flowers she tended and watch the birds hop about the grass and fly up into the branches. I'd scrunch up my body like an inchworm to navigate the lawn. At length I could stand, first by holding onto the couch or Grandmother's hand and then all by myself carrying my rabbit with me wherever I toddled. I had words now. "Rabbit" came out "Whoaboat" and soon was simply "Whoa." Grandmother spoke of him as the fourth member of our family and gave him a seat at the table. She took care of me mostly because now Mom was a secretary at Northwestern. We'd meet her at the train coming home.

I was an early talker. My first full sentence, Grandmother loved to inform me, came out when I was lying with Whoa in the back yard by her zinnias watching some tiny bug wander through the blades of grass: "There he goes with the sweetest little smile on his face." I had only just turned two. One day when I was three Grandmother took me to the village green where two older girls were playing house at the war memorial. I put out my hand as if holding a tray and joined them with "Would either of you like a martini?" Their mothers traded severe glances and my grandmother hustled me quickly away. When I got bigger she liked to tell me these tales, but I have no actual memory of them happening. It's like when a photograph proves I was wading in Lake Michigan with Mom holding me up. It's the picture that gives me the memory not myself.

My mother had started dating the man who was to become my stepfather. He was an archaeologist with the Oriental Institute and would soon be going to what was then the Kingdom of Iraq, a mostly blank, odd, pink shape in the atlas Grandmother showed me. That atlas remains but my first sight of that map does not, only the many times I'd studied it later to see where my mom was. Strange that I'd already learned words and kept them in my mind but the things that occurred back then I didn't.

Mom wanted everything in her life to change. How did I understand that my mother went off with this new man after they got married? Grandmother says I was at the wedding and the pictures prove it. I'm suited up in blue flannel short pants, white shirt, jacket and bow tie with white socks and patent leather shoes. I'm a happily smiling little boy gazing up at his beautiful mom and his new dad.

I was to be left with my grandmother for a few months at first while they went in search of antiquities. I have no memory of Mom and Poppa Henry saying their tearful goodbyes. Yet I do truly remember a chilly afternoon early in the spring of 1948 because my grandmother told me never to speak of it ever again, even to her and especially not to Uncle John, so I know I've held it only in my own mind for over seventy years and it must be true.

Grandmother had decided she'd try to light a fire in the fireplace to warm us up. It had been Grandfather Heath's job and then she'd left it to her sons and then to their wives. Grandmother was not good at practical things beyond her garden. Several times she singed her hair lighting the stove burners. But she was in charge of me now and it was an unaccountably cold spring day. With all the kindling sticks and crumpled newspaper she'd used the fire got blazing, but she'd forgotten about the damper and soon our little bungalow was filling with smoke. She dashed about flinging up the windows then bundled me into my winter coat and yanked me out to the front step and closed the door. This is where my memory actually begins. I still see it with my own eyes, the two of us calmly sitting there on the cold cement step as if nothing was wrong while gray smoke pours out the windows on either side of us.

In such a quiet neighborhood no one passed by to notice, and eventually all that smoke must have disappeared up into the blue sky. It was for me to protect my grandmother from embarrassment at her absent-mindedness. That was my task in the house I was to live in with her until at eighteen I went out east to college.

So my life had finally begun because what had my life been before I could remember it? Things eventually disappear but I've held onto what I can. I wonder how much ahead of me will be cluttering up my brain. I do find myself wandering into rooms not knowing what I've come to look for, yet I can remember the cement step and my grandmother as she was, quite a bit younger than I am now, and how safe I felt back then.

SEPTEMBER

The garden is weeping.
Cool rain sinks through the trees
as summer shudders gently to its end.
Leaf after golden leaf drops
from the tall acacia.
Amazed and weary, summer smiles
in its dying dream of gardens.
Yet it lingers awhile by the roses
and yearns for rest.
Then slowly it closes
its great tired-out eyes.

MOSTLY MY GRANDMOTHER raised me. Mom was Julie Blythe now and for the first years traveled a lot with my stepdad. It made sense for me to make my home with Grandmother and visit Mom and Poppa Henry at their apartment near Northwestern when they came back. "It's better than you being here and then there," Mom said. And when I was six she had Margaret, and after Henrietta came along they moved to their big Evanston house. Later the girls went with them on digs in Turkey and spent time in Syria too. I stayed on in the village so I wouldn't have to change schools.

I never called Eleanor Heath anything but Grandmother. Pop Henry, soon no longer Poppa, didn't officially adopt me, so I hadn't become a Blythe. The other young Heaths, Richie and Sally, came over with their parents for holidays and Grandmother's birthdays, but they had their own village now and Aunt Alicia didn't need to look in on Grandmother after Uncle John took over. He was also the man who oversaw my financial needs more than Mom could, and he deputized me to keep my eye on his absent-minded mother for signs of worrisome confusion.

To me she never seemed any different, though she did store away her heavy old record albums and the Capehart and switched to LP's. In time I inherited all her music and have trucked it around for five decades without listening to it much. I'm not prone to throwing things away. In high school Beau Templeton would kid me for that. We were still sort of friends, but he was with the athletic crowd I never felt at ease with. Then his mother got a bad cancer and I was the one person he'd ask to come hang out if he had to stay home to care for her. We'd be up in his attic room, Beau on his bed playing bluesy tunes on his guitar while I leafed through his Classics Illustrated comic books in the saggy armchair.

At home I still watched my grandmother bent over weeding her garden or sitting eyes-closed on the couch listening to her new LP records. There was one with a photo on the jacket of a kindly looking old man, nothing like the zombie-ish Rachmaninoff of my childhood nightmares. At the time I never really listened to it, but that record means something to me now because Grandmother wanted those songs played at her funeral. In what mattered to her she was not at all confused, but I did find her cigs left burning in ashtrays and the oven left on long after we'd cleaned up after dinner.

Naturally she developed cancer in her lungs and died two years after she'd seen me through Dartmouth where her first Matthew had also gone to college. I got a draft exemption for what our doctor attested was severe asthma because Grandmother couldn't bear for me to go to war like my dad and never come home. Beau had dropped out of Duke to join the Army and went off to Vietnam. His mom had died even before we took our separate paths to college, so we didn't see much of each other anymore.

Because Uncle John had plenty of money and my cousins were making good salaries by then Grandmother had seen fit to leave me a steady income as well as her house. After college I'd been drifting around New England waiting tables and clerking in small-town general stores, but I moved back home for her last months and stayed on awhile trying to decide what to do next. I didn't want to live in the village again, but I couldn't quite let it go. It turned out that Richie and his new wife Sondra wanted the house because it had also been his home once. I hadn't thought it meant anything to him, but he solved my dilemma by keeping it in the family. He gave me a fair price and I hitched a trailer behind my used 1962 Dodge Lancer and moved what I could to the little rooms I had in Montpelier, Vermont. It was late in the summer of 1968. I was then twenty-four and in another year would have outlived my father.

I don't want to think back to all those growing-up years. I don't want to remember my extended visits to Evanston with the girls and my mom in her new life. She was learning enough about Mesopotamia and Anatolia that Pop considered her a true partner in the field. Neither do I want to think about high school and the fooling around I did with other boys though never with Beau. I can't even dwell on the quiet times with the grandmother I loved more than anyone in the world. Aunt Alicia and Uncle John treated me as a somewhat sad case, the neglected son, practically an orphan, but I thought of myself as the lucky one. Grandmother loved me for being me, not as a substitute for her dead husband or her son killed in the war. I was an individual person of my own with all that made me Matthew Junior. That was enough.

But I do want to think back on the summer I turned twenty-five when I sublet my rooms to another waiter and went up into the foothills to a cluster of rough-hewn cabins and sheds to visit a former boyfriend and the girlfriend he'd decided he should be with instead of me. They called their community Elphinstone. Denny and Paula's cedar-shake cabin sat on the edge of a straggly old apple orchard. They had a pen for rabbits and a chicken coop and a mucky stable for their two horses. There was a dug well and a hand pump and a clawfoot bathtub beside an oil drum with a log fire beneath it to heat water. I could take a bath in the open with goats wandering about nibbling the long grass. A nanny goat would lean over the rim and bleat at me. Scattered across the hillside were other cabins full of artists and hippies and serious would-be farmers and various hangers-on. Denny wanted us to stay friends and figured it'd be good for me to see his new life and get to know Paula. I said I'd try it for a summer.

After a year of assassinations and ongoing war and violence in the cities and the death of my grandmother I needed a retreat. Staying with Denny wasn't the smartest move, but maybe up in the hills there was an alternative to the way the world seemed to be going. Everyone in Elphinstone acted cool about sex, but they called me "the straight one" because I didn't smoke weed. The day I arrived and introduced myself as Matthew Heath to a naked couple in the orchard tub the guy said, "Hey, man, don't be so uptight, mellow out, man." He was known as Tiger and his girlfriend at that point was a sweet kid he called Poochy. All these years later they reappear in my mind as if inside a morning mist in the cool Vermont June. I met so many folks that summer.

One day Denny saddled up the horses and put me on the shorter one. We were walking up a wooded trail to where a power line ran along the ridge when suddenly my horse took off at a gallop over the gravel road meant for maintenance vehicles. I'd never ridden more than a pony at the kiddie park, but I held on and didn't fall off when my horse pulled up to a sudden stop then turned around and shot off straight back to her stable. Being run away with like that put me more at ease for the rest of the summer. I had done something I'd never done before.

Denny Rourke was a short, brown-skinned, twenty-seven-year-old with such dark hair one of his diners once asked if he was Polynesian. "Just black Irish," he said. But he sometimes played on his intriguing looks for their mystique. He used to carry a copy of Knut Hamsun's *Pan* in his back jeans pocket, and later up at Elphinstone all he ever read was Hermann Hesse. I tried *Steppenwolf* and found it hokey. I wasn't much of a romantic despite having heard Grandmother's music in the evenings of my youth. Perhaps "romantic" isn't the word; "not much of a mystic" is better. The community in the foothills had its share of mystics with blurry visions of the future, another reason they saw me as the straight one.

I don't know what Denny had seen in me. I was tall and scrawny with wispy light-brown hair and leftover adolescent pimples on my cheeks and neck. He may have thought me ripe for conversion to his looser way of living, but I was looser than he was when it came to sex because I'd had more practice back in school and college and was good at it while it was all amazingly new to him and he was still trying to decide if it was boys or girls he liked best. Frankly, whoever was into Denny he was into too, especially when they'd stroke his long black hair. He wasn't a selfish guy but only more full of enthusiasms and dreams than I had ever been. We never actually broke up. He just backed away though we did sometimes still sleep together before he discovered Elphinstone. Paula had clerked in a resale shop in Montpelier and was ready for something new. I met her the night we all went swimming in the Winooski. Denny was naked, self-conscious me too, but Paula wouldn't get out of her knit dress, which shrank up embarrassingly when she climbed out. A bare-topped girl in a bikini bottom threw her a towel and she disappeared behind a bush. I went to tidy up the restaurant while Denny took her back to his place. I found out about it some days later. He thought I'd be glad for him and I tried to be, but it was one thing to have had lots of sex with different boys and another to have had a first boyfriend. It wasn't easy getting over Denny and following him to Elphinstone didn't help.

There were no other young men up there who would call themselves gay because it was 1969 and a few weeks before Stonewall happened, not that I knew of it when it did. If guys fooled around it didn't mean they were fags or fairies. It was simply being free. I did have some sex that summer, even once again with Denny when Paula went down to visit friends, but mostly it was milking the goats, gathering eggs, picking raspberries and wormy apples, and hanging out on people's porches.

One Elphinstoner named Anthony Garston had actually just published a book about "what's up with our generation," as he put it, "because folks out there seem damn curious to know." It was reviewed in some big papers and he got his photo in *Life* magazine, but they mixed up his caption with another young writer's, which bummed him out, though he acted as if he didn't care. He was sort of pretentious but basically sweet-natured. I never did read Denny's copy of Anthony's book from the shelf next to his Hamsuns and Hesses. Though Grandmother had played all her old records and Beau and Denny and my friends at college loved to read novels it strikes me that I don't have much feeling for either. I wonder if I've left myself out of certain joys.

I can't remember word-for-word the things Anthony Garston said about our lives when we talked on his front porch. I can only sum up how our talks went. Anthony, or Garston as the others called him, had the hippie look of curly mop, chin fuzz, wire-rimmed glasses, and sandals, but he didn't sound laid-back like Tiger or like Denny with his new vocabulary of "heavy, dude" and "far out, man" and "you dig?" Anthony didn't have a girl up there since he was only passing through, but claimed to have a number of former girlfriends to his credit. His book,

Victories in Defeats, was about thumbing across the country, a story inspired, he said, by *On the Road* and *Lolita*, neither of which I'd read but from what I heard it seemed an odd pair. Denny found Garston's book too intense. It bugged him that it got down on all the good things Elphinstone was trying to accomplish.

Anthony had told me he was a nihilist because there was no way out of the great American mess. "So where are the victories?" I asked him, and he said the lesson he took from Buddhism was that you could rise above defeat by not giving two shits. I do remember those words coming out of those thin lips between his faint mustache and fuzzy chin. I asked him why "two" shits, and he said because anyone could not give one shit but it took extra effort not to give two. I assumed he was kidding around though he hadn't cracked a smile. Yet I remember the back cover of his book saying it was "one hilarious ride into the freaked-out soul of the new generation." When Poochy asked him if there was going to be a movie version all Anthony said was "In your dreams, babe."

He had taken over a one-room cabin from an older artist who had gone to tend her dying mother. Anthony's life was unstressfully random, he said, which was somehow different from Denny "going with the flow." In my former boyfriend's case it meant we could sleep together that one last time whereas Anthony was like a monk who'd risen beyond his own body and was no longer seduceable. Poochy and several others of the women would have gone to bed with him if he'd asked, and so would I.

Instead I settled for long talks on his porch looking out at fading apple blossoms blowing off the gnarly old branches. Anthony could probably tell I was attracted to him despite his scruffiness. He wore the typical cut-offs and splotchy tie-dyed T-shirts and he smoked a lot of weed, but he didn't talk like the other heads, which may be why he liked talking to me as if we were the sole intellectuals in the community. Once he wanted to know how it felt not needing to worry about bringing babies into this world. I supposed it was "nihilistic" of me, I joked. "Whoa!" said Anthony. I can hear the way he'd say "whoa" whenever a new thought struck him. Denny might have said, "You just blew my mind, man," but Anthony only had to say "Whoa!" for me to know he'd experienced a revelation. I didn't mention that it was my old stuffed rabbit's name.

We talked about ourselves once having been babies and how it was impossible ever again to achieve that empty state of freedom from language and meaning. I said babies did know hunger and thirst and gas pains and took comfort from warmth and touch. Anthony came back with "And that should be enough for anyone." I'm trying to recall his voice. It had a familiar midwestern lack of accent, but he'd hitched all over in his young life and he'd lost a sense of home. If he had a home anywhere, he said, it was with a pen in his hand and a spiral notebook on his lap.

Then he wanted to know where I, Matt Heath, felt at home. It was difficult to answer him. After Grandmother died and Richie bought the house, I didn't have a home anymore. I already could tell that Elphinstone wasn't it, but I could never be a vagabond like Anthony Garston. I had begun to think it was time to stop waiting tables but also not to go back to some small-town general store. My cousin Richie had been urging me to invest some of the money our grandmother left me in one of his oddball business ventures. The latest was a small natural-lambskin condom factory on the northwest side of Chicago. They used an old-world secret family formula for curing lambs' intestines for their perfectly penis-shaped appendixes, and fat Italian ladies sat at tables sewing in the elastics. Back then it was only straight men who used condoms. I told Richie it seemed a particularly strange enterprise for me to have a stake in.

At Elphinstone I could get mail if I drove down to Montpelier for supplies and my subletting waiter friend passed it over. I hadn't been there for a while and had let Richie's offer slide. Anthony was the one person I'd told about it and he thought I should take it on. His free-wheeling sense of life taught him to make use of whatever came his way. "Use" was Anthony's big new concept. He was writing a second novel he was calling *Love Users* about the love-peace-freedom folks really only being in it for themselves. Elphinstone was a weird place for him to hang out if he believed that, though it was surely true for a lot of the kids up there. What did we know about ourselves in those days? The men still pretty much ruled, especially Tiger and another guy we called Bango for his prowess with women. Being into other guys was tolerated as long as you weren't too effete about it and it was considered cool to be occasionally lesbian, but the serious feminists had their own community on another hillside and I suppose most gay guys preferred cities.

Anthony probably figured I'd be a source of material for his new book. The things we talked about may have turned up in *Love Users* if it ever got published, but when I left Vermont I lost track of that part of my life, which must be why I'm trying to remember it now. It was the summer when I finally took hold of myself.

Anthony asked me once if I was active or passive. At first I didn't know what he meant, so he said, "You know, in bed." I'd never thought of sex that way, so I told him I wasn't one or the other, I just liked doing whatever we felt like. I think he said, "So you're both a hedonist and a nihilist!" Of course I wasn't really either. That I wasn't intending to breed didn't mean I thought other people shouldn't, and if I enjoyed having sex it wasn't self-indulgence so much as having physical fun with another male. Men playing sports had physical fun with each other without being called hedonists, and crusty old bachelors weren't exactly nihilists, were they? But Anthony loved making theories, so I let him.

When I asked if he'd ever slept with another guy he said he wouldn't know what to do with two dicks in one bed, so I laughed and said with some irony, "Mellow out, dude," and he admitted he was uptight in that regard and I'd better not get any ideas. It was the one time I felt hip.

But what was I doing up in those hills? If I'd somehow thought I'd get Denny back it was obvious it wasn't happening despite our one rematch in the loft where I'd been bedding down. I felt sorry for Paula because, from the lack of much bedtime activity downstairs, I could tell Denny was losing interest. There was a twenty-year-old girl named Katie who'd shown up halfway through the summer to get away from a bad boyfriend. Poochy, whom she knew as Patsy, had suggested she hide out at Elphinstone. Katie had a piercing stare as if she was trying to psych you out. I steered clear of her but Denny relished being looked at like that. He liked challenges, he'd say, which explained why my easy availability eventually didn't do it for him. I've always kept my yearnings to myself.

I wonder now if I was simply a shy and cautious young man who got uninhibited only in bed. When did I disconnect my bodily self from the quiet rest of me? It couldn't date back as far as being an unbothersome baby, but it might have to do with having been brought up by my grandmother and being the good grandson. I'd had to keep secret what would happen when I closed the door to my room, the room my dad and Uncle John had shared through high school. The dresser was placed so that if I pulled out the top drawer it blocked the door from opening, not that Grandmother would ever have walked in on me after I reached Junior High. I was her prize student, using Grandfather Heath's roll-top desk and wooden file cabinets and the shelves now filled with my textbooks and collections. I got top grades in English as well as in Math, but it was numbers I preferred. I wrote "excellent" papers on the books we read and remembered all the historical facts for tests, but in Algebra and Geometry I could be more myself, not trying to please anyone else but to arrive purely at my own solutions.

In one of our talks I tried to explain this to Anthony Garston, but he missed my point. He said I should also try writing a book because I was clearly smart enough. I told him I didn't have anything to write about. Yes, I'd been valedictorian in high school and got straight A's at Dartmouth, but I had no idea what I'd ever do with what I'd learned. All I'd done so far was wait tables and ring things up on a cash register. That's when Anthony recommended I invest in the condom factory. "It's a totally mad thing to do, and let me tell you, Matt, natural lambskin is by far the most pleasurable condom money can buy, not that you'll ever need one, you cocksman, but you'd be doing us hetero guys a favor." I'm making up what he might have said, but he did talk that way. He was already nudging me to get out of Elphinstone and find my own life, but I couldn't understand why his Buddhist monkishness was fostering capitalistic speculation or why he himself stayed on up there except to be like a worm in the apple.

Denny had come to distrust Anthony for showing up looking like one of us but acting so superior, and he wondered why I spent so much time out on his porch. And how did Garston get the artist woman's cabin with all her watercolors of sunlight sparkling through pines and maples or laundry flapping in a gentle breeze? Apparently Anthony had met her on his travels and probably had given her some sweet love, Denny suspected, but he'd better be moving along when she returned! They all referred to her as the Godmother of Elphinstone. I wish I'd met her.

Sometimes I'd see Anthony sitting under an apple tree barefoot and shirtless, eyes closed, so I wouldn't approach. It was too bad he wasn't up for sex because I thought it might enlighten him more than meditation, but that was just me. Not everyone was as devoted to that kind of relief as I'd been since age twelve, barring my bedroom door. Grandmother would be down the hall listening to her symphonies and she'd look up approvingly when I'd re-emerge as the self-motivated Matthew Junior who'd sequestered himself to struggle over the equations he'd in fact already solved between classes at school.

Once when they were home in Evanston from a dig in Iraq, Pop Henry took me aside to make sure I knew the things Mom was too embarrassed to explain and it certainly wasn't Grandmother Heath's job to tell me. Of course I'd figured it out for myself. Boys do have it easier than girls. In the days before girls were so available my schoolmates found it natural enough to experiment together when their families were out of the house. It was the same at Dartmouth with only an unsuspecting roommate to work around. In Montpelier it had been entirely easy in my rented room though I'd had a growing sense that it all might turn into something more, and it did for me with Denny Rourke. Now that was over. Up at Elphinstone I'd spent a couple of nights with one of the guys who was drifting through. We'd meet on a blanket in the orchard under the pin-point stars that cast no light. Later one of the serious farmers thought he'd give it a try, but it didn't work for him. Anthony seemed aware of these trysts and probably pegged me as one of the love users.

I wonder if having theories about everything in the universe wasn't a phase Anthony eventually grew out of. Maybe he gave up his writing because I've never heard of him since. I don't know either what happened to Paula after she broke up with Denny at the end of the summer. What finished them was his obsession for that Katie with the penetrating eyes. As far as I knew then it never went to actual sex, but one night in the cabin after too much home-brewed Newfoundland screech Katie launched into a loud rant about men being so fucking selfish and how she wasn't taking it so fuck off! It seemed she'd had a thing going with Bango. Suddenly she grabbed Denny around his narrow shoulders and tried to flip him. When they both stumbled and fell to the floor it turned into a crazy wrestling match twisting and flopping each other about. At the door Paula said Denny was a complete asshole and stomped out, but I was perched on the ladder to the loft and kept watching. The tumbling would take a breather and I was amazed that they'd kiss fiercely before getting back into the fight. It went on aimlessly, furious, drunken, fully-clothed: kiss, fight, kiss, fight, banging into the walls. Finally they were so exhausted they kind of passed out on top of each other. I crept up the ladder to my musty mattress and soon heard Katie prying herself off Denny and staggering out the door, mush-mouthedly saying he was the stupidest prick she'd ever run into.

Yet I did have some peaceful times at Elphinstone, not only lying out under the night sky or shooting the shit on Anthony's porch but picking raspberries by the bagful and milking goats and gathering eggs and eating all those meals we shared with other cabins, bread fresh from the wood-fired oven and river trout and goat cheese and all sorts of greens and sauces. There always was home brew to drink and pot to smoke into the sunset when I'd fill a glass of water at the pump and pretend it was screech. But I couldn't bear to watch while one serious farmer across the orchard shot the hog I'd figured he kept as a garbage disposal and strung it up to butcher. And I turned away from the bloody rabbits a weasel slaughtered in their hutch. But somehow I did like hearing coyotes howling at midnight. Maybe they'd killed one of the deer I'd seen passing silently through the woods behind our outhouse. There was wilderness up the hills from us where there were bears, which made me feel part of nature.

When we had dances among the old apple trees with candles strung up in paper lanterns and plenty to drink and smoke I tended to stand in the shadows tapping a foot and smiling and only reluctantly getting yanked onto the grass by Poochy who was determined to give me a good time. My body felt self-conscious dancing to that pounding psychedelic rock they played on a stereo plugged into a little generator. But I did at least grow accustomed to bathing naked in the tub with others coming by to hang out. That girl Katie cornered me once with her blue-eyed stare. "You don't really fit in here, Matt, do you?" she said not unkindly. And soon I made my decision to come down from the hills.

It had been my youth, I told myself strolling through the apple orchard on my last afternoon. September had arrived with colder nights and the gardens were beginning to die back and shrivel up. Fall came early at that elevation and now I was twenty-five years old. I did feel somehow still fond of that community spread out around me. I knew what it had meant to me, the last period of sweet deception in my life. It wasn't so hard then leaving Denny Rourke behind, so maybe I'd been right to live there and see him more as he was. I even felt a little sorry for him, but it was no longer for me to help him along.

We'd taken a long trail ride up at the power lines now that I knew how to keep my horse from bolting, and when we got to a crest with a nice long view we dismounted and took seats on a couple of boulders to eat our cheese and bread and raspberries and appreciate where we were. "So all this hasn't worked for you?" Denny said with rare wistfulness. I had to confess it hadn't. "No one else to fall in love with up here, huh?" I didn't think that was the reason but said I didn't regret the experience of having been in love with him. He said he was glad I was safely past it but probably hoped I wasn't quite. Denny came from a close family of brothers and sisters and a mom and dad and was used to being loved. I assured him I was fine and not to worry about me, not that he actually would, but I didn't say that.

So we looked out at the rows of hills in varying shades of green and blue-gray receding in the slanting sunlight. It was a mountain beauty I hadn't known before coming east for college and it had never quite felt mine. Katie was right that I didn't fit in, but Poochy cried and hugged and cried more when my time came to leave. Anthony only saluted from his porch sitting there Buddha-like, and Denny made as if he was sending me off on an adventure to the wild west. He wasn't given to compliments, but he did say I'd been of help figuring himself out. I doubt if he realized I'd been figuring myself out as well because he was always in search of role models with all the answers and I'd been one for a time.

According to a letter I got from Poochy years later Denny stayed on at Elphinstone well into the Seventies but then she lost touch with him. She was back to being Patsy and working in a nursing home in New Hampshire.

I drove my rusted-out Dodge Lancer down to Montpelier and the next day told my waiter friend he could take over the lease for good. I phoned Richie Heath to say I was driving back and would consider his capitalistic schemes when I got there. I might even take courses to qualify as an accountant because I had the math for it and could save him a ton on taxes. Richie had a good laugh at that.

Then I remembered Beau Templeton still over in Vietnam. I knew nothing else about him, yet we'd grown up together and he was the kid I'd felt so close to up in his attic listening to him plucking his twelve-string and humming a tune. Beau had the kindest soul, but he was across the world shooting at people and maybe getting killed like my dad. If I got home and learned he wasn't still alive I didn't know what I'd do. I might find myself wanting to retreat to the unreal world of the Green Mountains. But I hadn't ever gone back to my Louisiana birthplace and didn't suppose I'd go back to Vermont either.

And yet the next night at a motel outside Fairport, New York, I woke from a dream of dying gardens and maples and pines swaying in the frosty air and a wood fire burning in a cast-iron stove. Then I slipped back into sleep. I was halfway home already.

III

FALLING ASLEEP

Now that the day has tired me out,
all my yearnings, like a sleepy child,
shall embrace the starry night
as my dearest friend.
Hands, stop your fussing.
Brow, forget those thoughts.
Now all my senses wish
to sink themselves in slumber
so my unguarded mind
may go soaring freely
up into night's magical realm,
deeply alive in a thousand ways.

When I turned fifty I began having troublesome dreams. I live now where I lived then, in a house built after the Second World War, a "modern" house with lots of big windows in steel frames that open not up but out, a house all linear and flat rather than boxy and peaked like the rest in the village. Mine is set back in a shady yard fenced by high boards so only the garage is visible from the street. I didn't want a house like the Templetons' towered Victorian or a tight little bungalow like Grandmother's. And the fence keeps my neighbors from looking in.

It isn't quite in the village itself but to the west on land filled in over a swamp. Grandmother used to tell me how when she was a girl vagabonds would set up camp out here with horses and wagons and cook-fires glowing in the misty night. I'd had enough of my Evanston apartment life and of one particularly problematic not-live-in relationship with a man named Jim. By then in my forties I was ready for seclusion. My new house had been some architect's experiment built before the other lots were developed with the standard ranch houses and colonials. My neighbors had no idea if one of my various male visitors indeed lived with me, but no one ever inquired. I was the quiet middle-aged bachelor who didn't want to be bothered. Weekday mornings I'd back my Saab out of the garage and head for Edens Expressway then roll back in at dusk behind an automatic garage door. There's a privacy in suburban living I still find comforting. I had missed it in my city apartment with others' noises above, below, and on either side. But when at last I turned fifty in such total suburban silence I began to have those troublesome dreams.

By day I felt safe enough with my high-fenced yard and within the house an open-air atrium as in a Roman villa but somewhat Japanese in style, or in imitation of Frank Lloyd Wright: dark wood, yellow brick, gray tile, speckled gravel. It does briefly open out between two back doors to a thick stand of arbor vitae beyond a low limestone wall. And in what I call my courtyard sits a huge cast-iron frog spouting, when I turn him on, an arc of bubbling water into a shallow blue pool.

These enclosures have suited all my various selves: caretaking son to Mom and Pop, overworked accountant home from the office, and what Anthony Garston claimed was the nihilist-hedonist self deep inside me. It proved comforting to have not only all my own walls and gardens and trees and a board fence but also an interior bit of nature ideal for lustful cavortings in sun or starlight. It was as if the architect had designed the place with my particular needs in mind.

With Beau Templeton settled for good out in Colorado I hadn't seen much of him over the years. After all the miseries he'd seen in the war he had come home determined to finish his degree and go on to medical school. He threw himself into his studies and had emerged a steady-handed orthopedic surgeon with a residency in Denver where he stayed. I'd see him whenever he visited his dad and was also getting reconnected with one of his high-school sweethearts. It truly surprised me later when I was the one old friend he asked to be his best man. His other buddies had never really been that close, he said. I wasn't part of the rowdy crowd he partied with and I'd helped him so much during his mother's illness and saw the side of him, playing his blues up in his attic, that he never showed his teammates. The Army had grown him up, he said.

We were sitting in a booth at the Sweet Shop, now long gone

with all the other village shops I once knew. And then over our malted shakes and club sandwiches I decided I'd better first tell him I was gay in case it might matter. He said he'd sort of guessed it and did I think after his being in the war it would make any fucking difference? We'd been friends since our sandbox days, hadn't we? That gave me an idea for my best-man toast. I'd kept the rubber dump truck we used to play in the sand with. I figured I could hold it up for all to see at the wedding reception as evidence of our long-shared history.

Over the following years Beau and Helen would come back to see his dad and her folks, and once when I had a conference out in Denver I got to meet their three little kids. And we began exchanging occasional letters, scribbled or typewritten, the kind nobody sends anymore. Beau and I wrote about things we might not tell anyone else. To this day I've saved those letters and I imagine he's saved mine though our recent ones are filed online. I've followed his surgical career and he's followed mine in finance. I've praised his caring for people's bones and he's complimented me on filling people's pocketbooks despite his political distaste for money matters. I've even advised him on his own finances, but mostly we've confided in each other things more private. His marriage hasn't always been smooth, but neither has my series of short-term sleepovers.

I wrote him when a big latex firm was pressuring me to disclose our secret formula for curing lambs' intestines. I had long doubted the sustainability of that old-world operation with its steaming vats of guts from New Zealand and its heated vault of wooden dildoes that dried the excised appendixes before they went to the sewing ladies and the packaging boys. So I sold out to the big guys just before studies found that lambskin, though proof against semen, wouldn't keep out viruses. My cousin

Richie joked that I was a business genius for getting out of natural condoms in time to save my own "skin." But I was to learn much later that latex also has its limitations. The time came when I found myself agonizing about telling Beau my recent bad news out of fear it would turn him away from me forever.

On a bright day in May of the year I would turn fifty with the crabapple tree blossoming outside my study window I wrote him that a few months earlier I had run a high fever and had just discovered that my viral status had seroconverted to positive. I phrased it clinically to mask the extent of my panic and despair. But after a mere three days when I looked out my kitchen window above the sink where I was washing up a week's worth of dirty dishes there came Dr. Beau Templeton himself through the gate and along the garden path up to my front door. He gave me a hearty bear hug and said he'd hopped a plane right away to come and reassure me face-to-face that if I got on the newest meds right now the disease could be managed as a chronic condition and I'd be around long enough for us to be old men together, the way we'd been together as babies. No one had ever done me such a kindness, not even my grandmother.

But then soon after my birthday those nightmares began. I'd made it safely through so many years and yet despite precautions had at last been infected. In my waking hours Beau's reassurances kept me confident of continuing health, but sleep let loose a discombobulating tangle of fears and regrets. Eventually I wrote him about that too, and through his professional connections he got me a referral to a Dr. Mary Coleman. I'd never paid much attention to what passed through my sleeping head, but she soon had the two of us going over all that frightening nonsense to learn what it signified even if she couldn't alter the realities of my life. I don't want to remember any dreams now. Outside of a therapy session nothing is as boring as going over your own dreams. Mine explained certain things about myself that I've come to accept, and that seems to have been enough for me.

Gradually the worst dreams began to dissipate and soon being fifty wasn't so bad after all. The nights were becoming times to look forward to. I was getting intrigued with my own mental processes as if freeing myself from the haunts of death: my father's, my grandmother's, the death still to come of my mother, even my eventual own. When Dr. Mary asked why my old childhood friend's name kept cropping up in our sessions I told her how I'd watched him play his guitar while his mom was dying downstairs in her bed, the first time I'd seen what death might be like.

While I was seeing Dr. Mary old Pop Henry died and my devastated mother soon went to live in a residential community for retired academics. I saw no reason to tell her about the virus. Neither did I tell my half-sisters, but I did inform previous bedmates for their own sakes and counted myself lucky to be alive though it wasn't comparable to what Beau must have felt coming home safe from Vietnam. And then I went out and adopted my first dog.

With Dr. Mary's guidance my now gentler dreams seemed to be leading me toward something new. She was a short and scrawny woman about my own age with wispy dull blond hair and granny glasses as if she'd stepped down from the hippie hills of Vermont two decades ago. I began to sense whiffs of old Elphinstone hopefulness bubbling up in me.

Now that my nights were less marked by terror I discovered in them a nostalgia for things long ago. Grandmother's garden kept appearing and Dr. Mary also wanted to hear about the grandfather I never knew. I told her of the collections he'd left in his sons' room, the room that became mine. My dad had expanded my grandfather's stamp album with inflationary German stamps supposedly once worth thousands of marks and stamps from odd places like Tannu-Tuva and the French Territory of Inini. He and my uncle had played with Grandfather's lead soldiers, and by myself when I was little I'd played with them too. "Ah!" said Dr. Mary.

Her office on the edge of Evanston was in a blank brick building, a converted warehouse. Despite its thickly-painted cinderblock walls, pale yellow as I picture them now, the room felt cozy with a wall-to-wall brown carpet and soft Naugahyde furniture to sink into or stretch out upon. The walls were hung with soft-toned watercolors that could have been by the Godmother of Elphinstone. Dr. Mary was like a more trustworthy female version of Anthony Garston. I felt entirely safe with her, even when she wouldn't take my bullshit evasions.

"You miss your father, don't you, Mr. Heath?" she said once. She called me Mr. Heath and I called her Dr. Coleman except in my thoughts. I asked her how I could miss a man I'd seen for a mere two weeks when my newborn eyes couldn't properly focus. "Perhaps that's all the more reason to miss him," she said.

"Well, I may have lived fifty years without a father," I said, "but so have millions of others." She snapped right back with "Is that any excuse not to miss yours?" I accused her of being like one of those Christians who believes every child needs both a father and a mother, but she wasn't talking about every child, she was talking only about me. "Generalizing is one of your favorite dodges, Mr. Heath," she said, so when I got to my car I wrote those words down in the notebook I kept for recording my dreams.

Lately I've been pulling that notebook out of one of Grandfather Richard Heath's wooden filing cabinets that have accompanied me through all my moves along with the boys' adventure books heavily thumbed by my dad and uncle if not much by me, and the stamp albums, the lead soldiers, the mineral samples, the large geodes, the fossils of ancient ferns I collected on a field trip to Grundy County. Whenever I got home from therapy back then and saw my collections ranged on my study shelves, along with the Erector Set given me by Pop Henry, they seemed like historical artifacts and not merely the residue of various forgotten childhoods.

And there I've also kept the souvenirs Mom and Pop Henry brought back from distant lands, a shard of clay, a jewel-like stone, an iron blade. My mother had become a person she never would have been if Matthew Senior had lived. I never knew what it would've been like to have a mother always at home. Dr. Mary said that watching Beau losing his mother must have given me an inkling of what I had also lost. Not that Mom ever actually abandoned me. When they came home from their travels I always felt genuinely loved and respected for helping my grandmother and for doing so well in school and writing such grown-up letters to wherever they were, whether luxuriating in palaces or roughing it in desert tents. When Margaret and Henrietta were old enough to travel with them I may have felt a twinge of envy, but I told myself I didn't really want to visit strange and dangerous places, I wanted to stay home with all my things where they belonged. And I'd already learned to sequester myself behind my bedroom door after I'd secretly begun to explore the new sensations my body was suddenly capable of producing. If on her returns home Mom sensed me holding back my formerly enthusiastic welcomes she probably attributed it to adolescence.

I was more affectionate with my half-sisters, especially feisty little Henrietta with whom I'd sympathize whenever she got into trouble. Pop Henry never tried to interest me in his expeditions, but he always treated me kindly enough. It was only after he had his stroke in the mountains of Oman and came home to waste slowly away that Mom and I finally grew closer again. I'd pick them both up in my newer Saab and wheel him into my courtyard for a picnic, and Mom would tearfully apologize for all the years they'd left me behind. "But I've come out fine, haven't I?" I'd say, and she'd say, "But, but, but you're alone, Matty!" and I'd claim to like solitude too much ever to be a decent partner for anyone.

Soon it was she who was alone and I was still keeping my secrets from her though I did admit to being in therapy thanks to a nudge from old Beau. She'd always loved Beau and surely wished I could've been more like him. She would go on about us two tiny boys in the sandbox and poor dead Cathy Templeton and soon needed my hugs to soothe her tears.

Dr. Mary had heard all about my family, not that she could tell me what it added up to. That wasn't the point, she said. I should keep talking and she was there to prod me. As our mornings wore on I began to sense unfamiliar pulses moving about my head preparing me for what I couldn't yet identify, something waiting to be opened up like a birthday present. Somehow I wasn't afraid of the excitement. This time I wouldn't be falling for an impossible Denny Rourke.

My office colleagues sensed nothing different in me, not even Evelyn Grandy at the front desk who usually picked up on my moods. I've always guarded my inner self. Back with Denny I'd acted as if it didn't matter if I wanted him for anything more than sex. I never showed hurt when he asked me for some nights off.

Once he told me he just didn't feel like a man when we got doing the things we did. I told him he was being uptight: everyone should be and do what they liked being and doing with someone else who liked being and doing it too. Couldn't he be just plain Denny the way I was just plain Matt? Dr. Mary would let me go on about such things for a while, all the ways things were changing about male and female roles, before pointing out that once again I was dodging the specifics. But it wasn't easy telling graphic details to a straight woman. I suppose it isn't easy telling graphic details to anyone because they're what the body does on its own without recourse to words.

One time Dr. Mary got me describing my house. I even drew up a floor plan, which she found revealing. "Your enclosures are keeping you safe," she said. "They provide a private stage for erotic performances so you no longer need to seal off your bedroom with the top dresser drawer." "Performances?" I had to ask. But she wondered if I was as much doing it as watching it. "Definitely doing it," I said but suddenly wasn't as sure. I had a vision of Anthony Garston's Buddhistic smile, his lips opening to say, "You love user, you!"

Early one morning when I was acting particularly resistant to her questions Dr. Mary announced that what I should say to myself now was: "Oh, what the hell!" because I scarcely ventured out of my safe haven except daily to go to work and see her three times a week. And I was fenced off from my neighbors without having bothered to discover who they were. But now, she proclaimed, there was obviously something yearning in me because I kept complaining of restlessness, of itchiness, and of certain long-lost feelings I couldn't quite name.

Then one bright Indian summer day rather than backing my Saab out from under the automatic garage door to go shopping

I found myself walking to the front gate and stepping through onto the sidewalk. Neighbors seldom walked there, but that day a woman was just passing. I was so startled that we almost collided. I gasped then stupidly said, "We've hardly met, I'm Matthew Heath next door, well, I guess that's apparent." She gave a sly smile, introduced herself as Olive Sandstrom, and hoped her son's piano practicing didn't disturb me. I said I seldom heard it but when I did, out in the garden, it made me think of my grandmother who loved classical music and I trusted she wasn't bothered by my new dog's barking. Not at all, she loved dogs.

After nearly a decade of living on opposite sides of my fence we kept talking all the way to the corner mailbox where she dropped in a letter the way people regularly did back in the Nineties. Then she turned around toward her own ranch house and I pretended to have somewhere to go farther on. It was sufficient for a start.

Olive hadn't pried into my private circumstances and neither had I into hers. She soon went out of my conscious thoughts, but a few nights later there she was in a dream mixed in with my grandmother. The next morning in therapy Dr. Mary happened to ask again about all the women in my life. How did I feel about Beau's wife Helen? Or my cousin Sally who'd been a sort of big sister when I was small? And my half-sisters? Of course, I'd talked about all of them before, but each time Dr. Mary noticed something new in what I said. I'd named my dog Poochy after that girl in Vermont. Why? Then we finally got to Mom for the hundredth time and last of all to Grandmother. Did I still miss her? For once I didn't quibble. After all I'd sat by her bedside while she was slipping away from me. Naturally I missed her! How could I not? She'd never stopped loving me!

Then I mentioned the neighbor woman I'd just bumped into. "Ah!" said Dr. Mary in her knowing way.

That night I didn't stay late at work for once but drove straight home and right away gave Sally a call. What the hell, I hadn't seen my cousin since her New Year's Day tea when I brought Mom on her walker from the retirement community. Sally in her fifties was like Sally as a child, loud and enthusiastic and in total charge of her husband Samuel and their college-age kids. Her tall Victorian reminded me of Mr. Templeton's spruced-up house a few blocks over, but Sally's was a plain flat brown with overgrown hedges and an unpaved driveway. At her request I had brought my new dog. Samuel had allergies, but Poochy was a Schnauzer mix who didn't give off dander.

That warm evening we sat on their three-season porch and caught up on the extended family. I saw her brother Richie often enough on business but hardly ever the expanding brood of my cousins' kids or even my own Blythe nieces and nephews. Henrietta would come out from Chicago to see Mom and drop in afterwards to report. Before her divorce Margaret lived closer in the village but seldom came by, though we spoke on the phone now and then. But because Sally had also lived at Grandmother's when we were little kids I had decided to confide in her about my viral status.

Her first reaction was "Oh, Matty, but we always assumed you were celibate!" I didn't know what to say. They could never conceive of me rolling about in my moonlit courtyard on a blanket by my frog fountain with another naked man. To them I was a lone fellow of fifty, a sexless creature with a rescue dog and a tedious job. I suppose my looks contributed to the impression—my pocky complexion, my gangly frame, dull wispy hair, bifocals—and there I sat on their porch dressed blandly in khakis, a blue buttondown, and loafers. So I pretended I'd been involved in only one unfortunate short-lived affair, which was true except for the "one." Sally said, "What unfair luck!" and gave me a commiserating glance while Samuel stared at his knees. But at some point he said, "And to think you once owned a condom factory!" Poochy sensed my discomfort and hopped up onto my lap. Stroking her wiry black hair I assured them I was on the right meds and that these days it wasn't a death sentence.

We soon moved on to lighter topics. Sally kept saying how cute my dog was, and Samuel made a cautious move to pat Poochy's head, which she welcomed with a happy bob of her docked tail. Then Sally said, "Remember when we were little at Grandmother's and we'd ask her to do the owl, and when she did the owl we'd all scream and run away?" I said I was too young, so Sally explained that Grandmother would drop one eyelid without squinting and keep the other eye wide open like an owl. Maybe I did remember that.

When I left I asked them both not to say anything to Richie or my sisters about what I'd told them, and I'm sure they never did because in their small world it didn't fit with their notion of our family.

Dr. Mary was a bit taken aback by their reaction. Family may not be the best people to start with, she admitted. Not mine anyway, I added. But there was surely more to be said about them in therapy. So on we went, and it wasn't long before we arrived at yet another woman in my life: Dr. Mary Coleman. I know it's called transference, but I trusted my doctor's methods. She was teaching me a course on the subject of Matthew Heath, junior.

Olive Sandstrom and to a lesser extent her husband August had been becoming my friends. I'd had business colleagues and clients and numerous bedmates and of course my extended family, but aside from Beau out in Colorado I had no one as an intimate presence in my life. Hence the dog? In our later sessions Dr. Mary began taking an extra interest in this Mrs. Sandstrom. She found it interesting that my neighbor was slightly older than I. She remembered I'd once mentioned a stillborn baby girl. She speculated that perhaps when I'd learned of her in my early teens I developed a desire for a protective older sister to accompany me through my lonesome adolescence. I said I'd never thought of myself as lonesome. I had my grandmother, and Uncle John had looked after my needs when the Blythe family was abroad, and I did have school friends even if they only invited me over when their parents weren't home except of course for Beau after his mother got so sick. How could I know what being lonesome was, Dr. Mary wondered, if I had nothing to compare it to? "Children tend to accept what is," she said. I wrote that down in my notebook. "But now," she insisted, "it is our task to look back at what had actually been and what might've been instead." I didn't see why because it was too late to do anything about it. "If you're going to dodge me again, Mr. Heath," I remember her snapping at me and then not exactly threatening to stop working together but that was how I took it.

Yet I stayed on and for a while my loss of an older sister found its way into our sessions, but I wouldn't accept the notion that Olive Sandstrom was somehow an unconscious reincarnation of a stillborn baby. She was simply my new friend Olive. Once she invited me to come hear her son Hilding play his recital piece. At sixteen he was a pudgy-faced, fat-bottomed boy sweating nervously through a thunderous prelude by that fearsome Rachmaninoff and twice starting over in the most difficult parts. I found him rather touching, an earnest kid loved and admired by his parents and his piano teacher but with few pals beyond his sister Kristin who danced about gracefully in their sun room while he played.

Unlike her husband Olive is not of Swedish descent. Her genes like mine go back to various rural counties in England. She's somewhat stout and dark-haired like her son. It's Kristin who inherited August Sandstrom's elongated head with blue eyes and yellow hair like the flag of Sweden, he says. Their ranch house has some old-country touches: painted furniture, colorful crockery in open cabinets, faded photographs of somber Swedes, and an atmosphere of cultural seriousness and discipline. But Hilding was eager to play and Kristin to dance without any parental pressure.

After that visit I invited Olive and August over for tea, but by then winter was setting in so they couldn't appreciate the inactive frog fountain in my overgrown courtyard. With Poochy trailing us I gave them the house tour: from my kitchen of white porcelain and blond wood down the glassed-in corridor for a brief peek at the guest room and into my sparsely furnished bedroom then through the dressing room in the corner passage and on to my study where one window looked out at the cold fountain and the other at my hibernating crabapple. That room full of my collections and filing cabinets and my grandfather's old rolltop desk seemed not to belong, August said, to the rest of the house. "And what is that row of fat wooden pegs on the shelf above your desk?" he wanted to know. To anyone else I would have made up something about salvage from a bobbin factory, but looking at my friendly neighbors I didn't hesitate to amuse them with the story of the lambskin condoms and the drying vault of wooden dildoes and my good luck in having sold the business before it was too late.

So we all relaxed and I led them outside across the flagstones to the other back door and into the living room with its warming wood stove. Leaving them sitting uncomfortably upright on the Danish-modern couch I went to bring in the tea. Apropos of condoms we did eventually speak more soberly of the sexual risks out there these days, and before I'd thought twice about it I had told them my viral status. Immediately Olive said they had several friends in a similar situation and indeed had lost one to the disease before the latest treatments were generally available. If only he had held on for two more years!

The Sandstroms had obviously already figured out my sex life because Olive now said she'd hoped one of those nice-looking men she'd seen come and go through my front gate might prove permanent but she didn't mean to be a busybody. She had assumed I preferred my privacy and had awaited my cue. Having poured out more cups of tea and passed around a second plate of cinnamon toasts I felt we were becoming truly closer. Not since my days on Anthony Garston's front porch had I felt like that with someone new.

Dr. Mary seemed to perk up each time I told her of these afternoons that soon evolved into evening dinners. At night I'd fall asleep hoping for my next unconscious wanderings through territories I'd never known. I'd report these new dreams lying back on Dr. Mary's couch where I might let my thoughts roam more freely. It's impossible to convey the analytic experience to a skeptic, but something was happening despite the man I'd recently begun seeing who kept grousing about how it was only her way of scamming me into paying her to sit there and say nothing. But Dr. Mary and I eventually did in fact agree to terminate when I found myself getting more deeply involved with this man, Ezra Pomfret. It seemed wiser to venture into a promising new relationship without continually reporting on it. I should be "in" it, not "watch" it, said Dr. Mary. "We can always resume our sessions if you need to," she said, and I probably should have but never did. These twenty-odd years later I don't even know if she's still alive. That seems awful of me. Week after week we'd had the most personal of communions, if an unreciprocal one, but I guess that must be why it helped me so much even if Ezra said analysis was all crap.

The Sandstroms knew all our other neighbors and had thrown a party that year on Saint Lucy's Day for everyone on the block. Poochy was included and came as a surprise to most folks because I always kept her inside my board fence or drove her out to the forest preserve for her walks. The Bensons across the street brought their long-haired dachshund, and the two dogs entertained themselves at our feet while we humans talked and drank and ate. Kristin Sandstrom glided about with lit candles in her tiara, and her brother played soft pieces by Grieg on the piano.

Once there had been back yards full of screaming children and teenagers biking up and down, but the Sandstrom kids were the last of them, and I lived now in a neighborhood of older couples. There was a book group and a Mah-Jongg club and a bunch that got together to watch movies on the VCR. I was invited to all of these but only attended a few video nights. I should have hosted one myself but didn't yet have a tape player. And then came the inclusion of Ezra on one such evening at the Sandstroms'. They had us all over for a black-and-white movie from India called *Pather Panchali*. It was like no movie I'd ever seen. The sitar music brought tears to the brims of my eyelids. By the silvery light from the screen I looked at that big handsome fellow Olive had introduced to me as Ezra Pomfret and saw that his eyes were glistening too. He'd arrived alone. Olive explained he'd come out from Vermont years ago to work at a structural engineering firm in Chicago. Wisely she had not told me anything about him ahead of time, but I knew and he knew that she was making a match.

When I told Dr. Mary she asked what had made my tears well up. I stared at the sound-proofing panels of her ceiling and finally said it was the sad melody of the Indian music. "But what usually makes you cry?" she asked. I said I didn't often but I did at my grandmother's funeral when a violin solo in one of the songs she wanted played had soared up in a lovely melody. Dr. Mary kept probing. Could it only have been from the music? "It was my grandmother's funeral! Of course I cried!" But at the Sandstroms' party? I admitted maybe it was because of that other single man there with tears in his eyes, but I'd felt my own tears coming even before I noticed his. "And?" True, I had liked his looks. He'd reminded me somehow of Beau Templeton. I hadn't made the connection until I said it aloud in therapy. "And?" Maybe I just didn't suppose he was someone I could ever be with. "Go to bed with?" But that wasn't at all what I meant. It was that long-forgotten feeling I'd had for Denny Rourke but now turned into something not as young and stupid. And it was also a sinking sense of never, never, never. That's what I said. Dr. Mary asked what the movie was about, if that didn't have something to do with it, and I'm sure it did but I can't remember what because it was all those years ago and I've forgotten. I can only recall that it was awfully sad.

Soon I had begun seeing Ezra who was one of Olive's other friends with the virus, so we were reluctant to go to bed right away. We talked about it though, and that was fine because we had weeks to get to know each other first. He was a few years older than me. We'd certainly never crossed paths when I lived out in his home state. As a native Vermonter he hadn't appreciated all those communes sprouting up in the Sixties because that hippie life had seemed so unrealistic and self-indulgent. I found myself getting defensive of Elphinstone. But he'd gone to a technical college and like me had a mathematical mind that he applied to structures rather than bank accounts. He owned a condo on the North Side but was tiring of city life and the clubs and the parties. Myself I'd never gone much to bars or baths and found my partners in more intuitive ways, glances passing on the street, lingerings at shop windows, prowlings in parks. That was tiring too.

At that time, mere months into her widowhood, my mother's health was starting to fail, so I spent my last sessions with Dr. Mary on Mom. How did she figure in my dreams? I was no longer envisioning her with paralyzed Pop Henry out in my garden. Now she would appear in places I'd never been, deserts and crumbling ancient cities from her tales of travel and those postcards and photos I've saved of sites like Palmyra and Kish and Uruk. In my youth I must have conceived of my mother's life as something magical out of an adventure book I'd never get to read.

When I was in high school her old friend Barbara from their army days had come for a visit with all the Blythes. She found me alone on a Saturday afternoon sitting on the stairwell windowseat in the big Evanston house doing my math problems, and she sat down beside me to talk of good old Julie. Barbara had always figured Mom was keeping something private inside her. Sure, Julie would drink and smoke and swear along with the other gals, but she never would quite let go. "Your father's death must have broken her loose," Barbara said. "Not that she didn't love your dad, oh man, hell no! But what with her own mother's constant pissing and moaning about her divorce Julie couldn't see hunkering down there where she'd grown up. Who knows if Matt could've taken her away, but look at your stodgy Uncle John, Matty! Don't you get like that, stuck here being so responsible!" That's the way Barbara talked.

And in my fifties my dreams of a magical mother kept coming back though soon Ezra was getting mixed in too. A robed woman was on a spiritual quest passing in bright sunlight through a ruined temple, or she was in a small boat like the eight-foot pram Ezra was building to sail on the lagoons in the forest preserve, but it was on a Turkish sea at sunset and at the tiller was a female figure. Dr. Mary asked if maybe the robed figure was also myself up there steering the boat. At first that seemed absurd, but isn't everything in dreams a part of your own psyche in various disguises? No, I'm not going to mull over my old dreams anymore.

Though we had not yet done more than hug and kiss it was a help to have Ezra with me when Mom was dying. I kept seeing Dr. Mary through those last days, but it was hard to pay attention to my therapy with all that was changing around me. Margaret and Henrietta and I were suddenly spending much more time with each other, and their kids came and went from their grandmother's bedside too. Mom was exactly the age I am now, approaching seventy-four, not yet seventy-five, far too young, but to her grandchildren she must have seemed ancient. She'd lost her first husband in a war they read about in school. She and their grandpa Henry had lived in places armies were still fighting over. The kids would take hold of Mom's hand and try to get her to say more about the past, but mostly she just murmured how much she loved each of them and made a soft smile or a wink that was likely involuntary.

Ezra often came with me, and one of the last things Mom said that I could make out was "Now you'll be happy, Matty." And with Ezra she simply squeezed his hand and said, "I'm so glad." I recalled sitting for those many days beside my dear grandmother's bed. It didn't seem all that long ago. I still comfort myself that unlike my dad's death in battle, or Pop Henry's paralysis, or even what Mom reported of her own mother's excruciating last months that I at age ten had not been allowed to witness, and how she didn't even know it when her father died in some Chicago drunk tank—unlike all those deaths my grandmother and my mother managed to slip peacefully into the oblivion we all have to accept whether we want to or not.

Aunt Alicia came to keep us company and seemed pleased to be outliving her sister-in-law because she knew Grandmother had always preferred my mom. I felt a little sorry for my aunt. Uncle John was taking care of all the arrangements so we wouldn't have to. Richie and his family, Sally and hers, they also came and stopped by my house after the funeral to make sure I was doing okay. By then they did know about Ezra and took note of all his tons of stuff piled up in the guest room. Step by step he was moving in.

IV

THE RED SKY OF EVENING

We have gone hand in hand
through joys and sorrows,
and we both want to rest now
in this quiet land.
Valleys bow down around us.
The air is already darkening.
Only those two larks climb up,
dreaming of night, into the dusk.
Come here close to me
and leave them to their whirring.
It will soon be time for sleep.
We must not to lose the pathway
in this lonesomeness.
Silent peace spreads far beyond us,
deep under this reddening sky.
We have grown so tired of wandering.
Is this something like death?

I'm in my study at my old desk, the desk my grandfather used and passed on to his sons, and then it followed me out here to my enclosures. I'm staring out the south window at my crabapple tree with no hint yet of any buds. Slanting sunlight from the west strikes my shelf of wooden dildoes and throws a dozen long shadows like bars of a cage across the opposite wall.

I have pulled out from a bottom drawer the neatly folded forty-eight-star flag my Aunt Alicia received from the soldiers on Grandmother's front steps back in the spring of 1945. It lies on my desk now, white stars and dark blue sky, one of my many treasures. Grandmother never could look at it. She'd asked my aunt to wrap it in paper and give it to my mother to keep safe for me. Mom couldn't bear to unwrap it and forgot to pass it on until after Pop Henry died and she'd sold their house and retired to her apartment. I am the only person who has set eyes on it since the day it arrived at my grandmother's door.

When I first brought it home I set the package on my dining table, carefully unwrapped the paper, and unfolded the flag like a tablecloth. It looked unfamiliar after all those years of a flag with fifty stars. After folding it back up in proper triangular fashion I decided not to wrap the paper around it again and carried it to my study and laid it in a bottom desk drawer. Once in a while I'll take it out and think about it. It was not burned with whatever was returned from France with my father's body. His ashes have been in an urn in the church wall ever since I was a gurgling baby in my mother's arms.

Mom was full of guilty apologies when she passed the flag on to me, but I assured her I understood. It's hard to part with things. Look at Whoa the Rabbit. Poochy had somehow gotten hold of the overloved thing and worried him into shreds that I now keep in a plastic bag in the desk drawer where I've stored the flag. But Mom had found that fact far too sad and began to sniffle again. I didn't really mind about Whoa, I said, because having Poochy made up for it. "If only Poochy were a person, Matty!" said Mom.

I'm glad she later came to know Ezra and could imagine me happily accompanied after she was gone. That's how I wish I could leave it too. I certainly don't care to think about my two-plus years with Ezra Pomfret. It would only be a series of wishes and hopes and disappointments and misunderstandings and missed chances, all the sadder because it had once seemed so possible.

So I'll dwell on certain memories but not all of them. Why should I have to remember everything? It's the turning points I've been thinking of. Approaching seventy-four I find myself at another one. It's not only that I might cut back even more at the office or move away somewhere warm the way Ezra did or even that I might get sick and start facing death. This new turning point is largely inside me. It's a weirdly fuzzy feeling at the top of my spine, something to do with the passage of time.

There sits Malinda, my aging second dog, staring up at me with her blackberry eyes. It's a red sky out there now, and she knows it will be dinnertime soon after her walk. Food will be her reward for having pooped. She's a yellow yard dog. I picked her out at a shelter when I at last got over Poochy's death. Poochy was a stubby little thing that somehow reminded me of my stuffed rabbit. Ezra had never been too fond of her and made me promise we'd never bring another dog into our life when we'd finally be free to take long trips together to faraway places without worrying about an animal. In our time together I let Ezra go on trips by himself unless we could bring the dog along in the car. Even after he moved permanently out to Santa Fe, leaving me and Poochy, whom I pampered until she died, it was a good eight years before I was ready to adopt again. Did I think Ezra might return?

IT'S SHORT-TERM MEMORIES that people say are what go first, so I'm trying to hold onto them before they fade. I don't want to think back too far. It's true that I recall the first months after Ezra moved in here more vividly than all these years after he left. I'm not even quite sure if what I did last week is not what I did the week before. Oh yes, Henrietta came by now that she's a grandmother for the second time to show me the latest baby photos on her phone. She didn't want to send them because she prefers watching me seeing them in person. She doesn't really approve of life being reduced to electronics, but for me it's somehow insulating. I can still picture Henrietta as I like to think of her. Not that I object to my youngest half-sister coming to visit, but when she was here in the flesh I couldn't quite take her in, a woman well into her sixties, because a smaller, smoother body kept shining through the surface of her present self. And with her phone's bright screen scrolling through tiny faces and tinier hands and Henrietta pointing out resemblances to various Blythes and Heaths—Margaret's eyes, Sally's chin, even something of our mother—I imagined I saw it all too. I could tell she was pleased.

But had she dropped in solely to show me her latest grandchild or was it her excuse to come check on me? She kept looking over at sleeping Malinda, no doubt envisioning the day when the dog would be gone and then what? "Matt," she said with a questioning lilt to that one syllable.

"Yes, half-sis." I'd used my comforting big-brother voice.

"You still seem perfectly happy in your life out here," she said. I remember it as a statement to reassure herself.

So I told her that, yes, I'm happy, I have my health, I'm part-time at work now, I have more than enough money, I have dear friends and colleagues, I have my loving family even if I'm not quite the doting uncle I ought to be. I've been lucky, unlucky in love perhaps but lucky in other sorts of good fortune.

Henrietta said she never had liked Ezra Pomfret that much. She figured he didn't get me, the way I actually am. She wishes she could be more like me and accept things as they are instead of constantly pushing against them. She's gotten better at it, she said. But how had I as a boy managed to learn that secret to life? It has taken her all these years!

Then we told stories of old squabbles with her sister and with her dad and how back then she counted so much on my funny letters to buck her up. And she reminded me of her standing offer: if ever I did feel too isolated I could come move in with the two of them in Chicago now that their daughters are out of the top floor. I'm the oldest relative she has left around here. Margaret has moved off to California to be near her kids' families.

It was nice to know that Henrietta is willing to look after a decrepit old me, but I know I'll never take her up on it. I have no desire to live anywhere else and no thoughts of traveling either. I never did go see Ezra in his desert life though for a time we communicated regularly on the phone and then by occasional letters. He did visit back here once in a while and we were fine with each other. At our age what did it matter? He slept in the guest room with the door closed. Olive and August were always happy to see him. He was nice to Malinda when she was a pup. But it's been some years now since I've seen him. I'm lucky that Beau and Helen come back here often to see her siblings and not that long ago to look after her aged parents and old Mr. Templeton who died at ninety-six, fifty years alone without his Cathy.

I admit I made Ezra restless, I know that. I'm happier at home and don't have much of a yen for other places. Our first year Ezra went off on his winter vacation to the Southwest and the next to a Caribbean island. He'd come back relaxed, so I didn't mind his going. I never worried that he might stumble into a substitute romance when we were apart. None of that seemed to mean much anymore. Strange how I once took such delight in letting my body play with another man's body. It happened much more easily than straight people might imagine even when the other man sometimes was straight, if not entirely so. When it comes to their bodies men know how each other's works, so doing things together can come quite naturally. Not that I have had any experience with women to compare it with. Dr. Mary Coleman would say I'm generalizing again.

Beau and I would sometimes come close to discussing such questions in our letters if he'd been having a rocky time with Helen. "I just don't understand women!" he'd write. I've never had to say that about men, at least not as a category. Beau would joke that he envied me especially after Ezra came along, so it took him by surprise when after not much more than two full years I had to write him that Ezra was moving out to Santa Fe for good. Beau had very much approved of him and so had Helen, and they wondered if there was any chance of him coming back.

Then Beau got angry, angrier than I felt myself, and he said it made him truly more grateful for Helen even when he didn't understand her at all. But I knew he had simply been able to adjust himself to another person and I hadn't. I'm thinking now of Beau growing old out there in Colorado still with his wife, with their kids and their kids' spouses and grandchildren up in Boulder. I don't worry about him the way I did when he was in Vietnam and I was hiding out in Elphinstone where I didn't belong. We're both safer now.

But here I am, sorting through the past when I haven't meant to. Malinda has padded in and flopped onto her bed in the corner. Now that she's old she has a bed in every room. She sleeps much of the day and all night curls up behind my knees in the big bed. Maybe the fuzziness that's crawling up my spine is the fear that she'll not be with me much longer. I'm not sure I'll be ready to start all over.

Beau once wrote me that aging is only another chronic yet manageable condition. I'm one of the lucky ones and he and I will be old men together, if a time zone apart. Ezra is healthy too. Out in New Mexico he hikes and plays tennis and goes to galleries and shows and the summer operas. It's a life he didn't have time for here while he was working. Maybe I'm still going to the office only so I won't have to do other things. I don't even know what they would be. Gardening is one activity, but it's mostly just clipping and weeding. I haven't made the hobby of it my grandmother did. And I have been painting all my interior walls in brighter colors over the cold whites. Thanks to the Sandstroms I do listen to more music now. August was intrigued by my shelf of inherited vinyl records and even more by the stash of heavy breakable ancient albums in the cupboard below.

A few months back he and Olive stopped over on an evening

when I happened to be playing the songs Grandmother wanted played at her funeral. The record jacket has a black back and no liner notes inside, so I didn't actually know beyond the title what I was listening to. I'd always taken the kindly old gentleman on the front cover as an incarnation of my dead grandfather, but he was actually the composer Richard Strauss, nearly eighty-five years old, and the songs were the last ones he ever wrote.

"Aha, Elisabeth Schwarzkopf," August said approvingly, "and wasn't she a beauty!" He pointed to the smaller photo of the singer I hadn't thought much of before. August said he'd email me a translation of the poems so I'd know what they were about. Until then I had only felt them as sad melodies I couldn't hum along to but they reminded me of evenings on the couch with my grandmother when I was a boy. They sent me back to that never-ending dream time I must have had down in Leesville, Louisiana, before I could hold onto anything from moment to moment, or I'd envision my grandmother with her head leaning against the couch cushion, her eyes closed, listening. It set me wondering about my life and how I didn't know what it had possibly added up to, starting with that view out the chicken barn's window right up to now looking out at my crabapple tree with its tight little buds not yet opening.

I've told my colleagues I'll retire for good when I reach seventy-five. It will then be fifty years since I came down from the mountains and went in with cousin Richie on the condom factory. I've certainly earned myself plenty enough since then.

Beau Templeton has attitudes about money. His eyesight is dimming, so he doesn't practice medicine anymore though he consults with young doctors and continues to raise funds for rehabilitating our recent veterans. He and Helen have always lived modestly. When I went out to Denver I found them crammed with three small kids into a one-story tract house, nothing like the cavernous Victorian he'd grown up in. The war did it to him, he said. He took no pleasure in luxury. Helen wasn't happy about that, but she adapted and loved him anyway. Beau used to dig at me for my lifetime of managing suburban money. In our letters we'd squabble over politics, but I concede I've never had quite the firm convictions he holds to. True, I've generally supported progressive causes, but our friendship went through a bad spell just last year over Sanders and Clinton. I said I was thinking strategically and he was being too idealistic. Even today he maintains that Bernie could've won the election. I suppose that old hippie senator made me think too much about my Vermont days and at least Hillary was from Illinois.

But there is one political notion he gave me that I'm most grateful for. Shortly after Ezra moved away Beau pointed out that I had enough cash to be able to spare some. He coaxed me to start giving my money away, moderate gifts at first to his veterans' charities, but then he wondered if I didn't have any causes of my own. It got me thinking about my childhood, about not having my mom around much and being in a certain sense an orphan. I thought there must even now be boys whose families unlike mine threw them out for doing things that came naturally to their young bodies and there must be organizations that need funding to help them. Beau referred me to several people, just as he'd found me Dr. Coleman. I began to write more checks. I even set up an independent account I could draw from and keep track of my donations and easily calculate my tax deductions. And I also put money into no-kill animal shelters. Why hadn't I thought of that earlier? Was I afraid to be left with nothing?

Now that neither of our candidates is president, Beau and I can unite again in our despair for the nation. That's another topic I spend far too much time dwelling on: newspapers, TV, the internet. I try to supplant my fears for the future with distracting memories of times I was in bed with another man, or two of us were out in my courtyard under the sky, or back in my Evanston apartment despite neighbors behind the walls, or even longer ago in my youth. It becomes all the more vivid the farther back I remember. I also spend many an hour with Malinda, who's named after the older sister I never got to have. Dr. Coleman was right to ask about the women in my life. They're probably why I preferred Clinton to Sanders. But what I try not to think about too much is Ezra Pomfret with all his clutter packed up in his U-Haul driving off that early morning nearly twenty years ago.

This is my life right now and it's reasonably stable, so why am I continuing to puzzle over it? I've become quite used to living alone again. The house except for my study is back to its spare simplicity. Day by day the only living things I have to accommodate are my plants and my dog. What I owe to the office I now do on my own time when I choose to. As for my relatives I see them on birthdays and holidays and occasionally make or receive visits to keep up with their news and pass along whatever is new of mine. I don't find myself bedmates much anymore, but I do have my nextdoor neighbors. We see each other coming and going and often get together to talk, eat, watch a movie, or walk Malinda.

Hilding Sandstrom recently stopped by with his wife. His musical ambitions haven't taken him beyond his position as accompanist for various North Shore choruses. His wife, as chubby as Hilding is, sometimes sings solos. I haven't seen his sister Kristin for a while. She's still spindly but got safely past her eating issues in college. She teaches dance at a suburban ballet studio and has an equally narrowly built husband who's an acupuncturist. Not having to act the uncle with them, I appreciate the Sandstrom kids as fellow adults. My actual family thinks too much in terms of generations. I've certainly never yearned for offspring yet have treasured the wooden cradle my grandfather built. I store logs and kindling in it beside the wood stove.

And of course there's still Beau. With his poor eyesight he doesn't even drive anymore. He enlarges the type to write me and also when my emails come to him. It's been tough to give up the precise work of his hands, but Beau is not one to stop helping people. He will be coming back here soon with Helen to stay at her older brother's house in the village. I'm looking forward to seeing my oldest friend as much as I'm also a bit anxious. I've felt more at ease in our letters. Face to face we both tend to be reserved, not to show too much affection. When he flew out to reassure me about the virus and gave me that heartfelt hug it seemed out of character for both of us. We quickly went back to our separate selves, but that hug sticks in my mind more than nearly all I've given or gotten since.

Perhaps when he visits we'll start talking as what he called "old men together" with no more need to put up a front. I'll fetch him at Helen's brother's and drive him out here in my new electric Leaf. I've given up Saabs. Because I never drive long distances I figured why not go electric. I'm even looking into solar panels for my roof, not so much for economy or ecology but to be more self-sufficient. These recent notions to separate myself from all that's out beyond my board fence, to choose when to see other people, to live simply without Ezra's clutter, to cut back my activities—it must indicate something else still to come. I've even begun to think about parting with some of my collections. I distributed Grandfather's lead soldiers and adventure books among the family's younger boys, but I couldn't give up the stamp albums or the samples of minerals and the fern fossils and geodes I found as a kid. I did let Ezra take the Erector Set. As for that row of wooden dildoes, who'd want them? Richie for a laugh? But he's likely to be dead before me, in and out of chemo as he's been. As for the treasures from the Blythe expeditions they can go to Margaret who helped collect them. Henrietta wouldn't care much for them. She hated those years of traipsing through deserts.

What I truly treasure are the relics of my dad, the shreds of the rabbit he gave me before he went to the war and the forty-eight-star flag that accompanied his body home. I'll have them burned with me and their ashes mixed with mine. They'll end up in an urn in the church wall next to my dad's and my grandparents', but I wish they could be scattered in the forest preserve. Before the C.C.C. drained that stretch of swamp into lagoons and my neighborhood got filled in by developers my grandmother could stand in her garden at dusk and make out distant campfires flickering through the rising mist and shadowy forms of wagons and grazing horses encircling the flames with mysterious human shapes moving to and fro.

Out beside one of those lagoons is where I first lay with another boy. We were in eighth grade and didn't have to think much about what we found ourselves doing. We had each separately discovered things our recently enlarged parts were ready for and wondered what we could do with them together. Hidden in a tangle of bushes by the muddy water with its croaking frogs we found there were lots of things. Then we biked back to the village and bought Pez dispensers at the Sweet Shop. I still keep mine in my pencil drawer. It was a happy way to begin a sex life.

I'VE CAUGHT MYSELF going off into the past again. It's useless to spend the onset of old age mulling over all that has been. There's something from last weekend that's still fresh in my mind, a visit from my cousin Richie. He's seventy-five now and retired from years of financial shenanigans, boom and bust and boom again. Once he had to take a clerk's job at the village hardware store to keep him and Sondra afloat. But he made some savvy investments and put himself back up where he'd been without having to sell whichever of his houses he had at the time.

Houses mean so much to people. I must remind myself I'm lucky to have one. Ezra has a little adobe one up a hill in Santa Fe stuffed with artwork and hangings and clay pots from the galleries out there. I've seen his virtual tour and can picture his new life without needing to travel. He likes it when other retired old folks join him in the shade of his patio, new friends he's made and some he got to know back on his first winter vacation. To them I must seem a mere figment of his past life.

Childhood time used to pass so slowly that I can recall a certain long-lasting Squibb toothpaste tube, a single bar of Cashmere Bouquet soap in Grandmother's bathtub, or my personal box of Post Toasties and that tall blue-and-white two-gallon canister of Jay's potato chips. Today I'm unaware of the brands I choose, replacements go unnoticed, supplies come in and go out with no resonant associations. An old fight with my cousin Richie over who got to help Grandmother blow out her sixtieth birthday candles is still there like a home-movie scene. But in recent years family times with Richie and Sondra have fused into a blur beyond any particular significance. But because he came over here last Sunday by himself, ostensibly to see how I was doing, I can still recall what we said before it merges with other such visits and I get stumped asking, "Now how long ago was that? November? August?" No, it happened in the last days of winter.

I had taken a short nap while the warm midday light could still reach me on the living room couch. I thought I heard a sharp knock at the front door but half-asleep decided I'd dreamed it. Then I heard footsteps coming alongside the house. I'd barely sat up to see who it was before the unlocked back door swung open and there stood Richie Heath in his red-and-black plaid wool jacket stomping his hiking boots on the mat. I said something like "Well, if it isn't!" and he said, "Hey there, cousin, thought I'd make sure you weren't up to some new mischief." He wriggled out of his jacket and warmed his hands by the wood stove.

Unlike cousin Sally, who'd thought I was celibate, Richie has always known of my lively pre-Ezra bachelor life and likes to rib me about reverting to it, though I seldom have. He takes weirdly vicarious pleasure in painting me as a free spirit and himself as tied down by Sondra and their offspring. He figures gay men get to carry on with other men the way straight men only wish they could with women, but women don't put up with that shit, he says. And most gay men, I've explained, don't even need to be seduced because they're generally equally horny. Maybe we're simply more essentially male, Richie, get used to it! But he always brings it back to how, shit, Matty, someone has to take responsibility for stabilizing society and providing a next generation.

That old theme didn't arise last Sunday. I went to heat up hot water for tea while Richie explored through the dining room and kitchen and on down the glassed-in corridor, where he stood looking out at the just-thawing pool below the frosty cast-iron frog. I brought him his mug, but instead of turning back toward the living room he moved right on into my bedroom where Malinda was asleep in her corner. She tried to make up for missing his arrival by going especially waggy and shadowing him on his tour all the way to my study. There, steaming mug in hand, he looked around as if continuing to evaluate the premises.

I took a seat at the desk, pondered the twisty branches of the crabapple tree outside, then spun my chair about and pointed him to the reading chair by the courtyard window. I felt the sunlight on the back of my sweater and knew I was silhouetted where Richie couldn't make me out as well as I could focus on him. I noticed his eyes shifting to the dildo shelf. All it took was a thumbs up and a sharp snort to bring us both back to our innocent natural-lambskin days.

"Where would you be now, Matty, if I hadn't dragged you into that investment? And then I let you buy out my share. What a sucker I was!" He's been saying such things over the decades. He likes to take credit for whatever solidity I've achieved. I'm willing to acknowledge his usefulness even though he'd been a nasty little kid to me. He claims he rescued me from penniless hippie decadence and I throw back that my life actually turned a good deal more decadent after Elphinstone. "Merely belated sowing of oats," Richie has said. I can't count how many times we've gone over our contrasting histories.

"So!" said Richie from the reading chair where he'd picked up a picture book off the side table, a guide to breeds of dogs. As if she sensed its contents Malinda padded over for a stroke or two, which Richie supplied absent-mindedly while with his other hand he flipped the pages. "Dogo Argentino!" he exclaimed, "I want one of those!" There is such a dog. I'd noted it as well. Then down went the book, up came the mug of tea, a sip, and Richie said we had to talk seriously about the future. That's a switch, I thought and awaited whatever was coming.

He reminded me that we weren't going to be around forever and while he had his legacies all properly laid out for Sondra and the kids and grandkids I had no direct heirs but my half-sisters. "Correct?" "Yes," I said. "Put in writing?" he asked. "Well, no, but I assume Henrietta and Margaret will automatically inherit my estate." "No Ezra Pomfret?" I told him we had settled our accounts when he moved away. "So you're quits," Richie said and added, "No sentimental anything?" I shrugged off the notion. Next he wondered if I wasn't keeping some young man on the side, but I've never been interested in younger men, I've preferred equity in bed. That brought a disbelieving grunt from cousin Richie. I used to hear rumors of his flirtations with young women at his firm, so I understood his skepticism.

Finally with a glance at doting Malinda he asked if I was continuing my charitable bequests. "Animals? Gays?" I told him I had already established discrete funds no longer included in my estate and had taken the proper deductions. Why was he asking me all of this now? Of course it was because he had just finished another round of chemo and was thinking about death. It was stupid of me not to have been better attuned to what he was going through. I suppose because modern medicine has mercifully prolonged my life I'd assumed it would also prolong his. "But shit, Matty, we're in our mid-seventies," Richie said briefly crestfallen.

Still I had a sense there was something more on his mind. From the way he'd been checking out the house it must be something to do with property. Sensing my sudden defensiveness Malinda had padded over to my side of the room. Richie said, "At least you'll outlast that dog." Annoyed I asked straight out if he was concerned about my real estate.

"It's a house that wouldn't suit most people," he noted, "but it might be ideal for my John and Hiroko now that their sons are grown." Richie had sold Grandmother Heath's bungalow long ago, and after several subsequent profitable deals he and Sondra now live over in Mom's retirement community, so my house—"mid-century, quite high value these days, Matty,"—was the one piece of Heath property that might be passed down in the family. He wanted to propose that I designate it for my first cousin once-removed, John Heath II, at a fair assessed value to be paid to my half-sisters.

Young John had never shown any interest in me or my house. To get off the subject I remarked how encouraging it was that my Uncle John having been stationed in Hawaii repairing fighter planes to bomb Japan had lived to embrace a Japanese granddaughter-in-law. Richie smiled at that then said, "Personally I've always wondered why after the Germans killed Uncle Matthew our grandmother wanted those damn German songs played at her funeral!"

My cousin was now sitting at the edge of the deep cushion where I liked to snuggle with Malinda and read to her about all the different dogs in the world. I did promise Richie I would make a lawful will but wasn't at all inclined to include a provision about my house. That was that. What if Henrietta's girls wanted the place? What if in Richie Heath style his son John simply turned around and sold it at a nice profit? I can't determine what will be done after I'm dead. My cousin has forever been on the lookout for sweet deals, and I've never fully trusted him.

So he shook his head as if I was missing out on honoring the family name by letting this architectural treasure go to some Blythe or Blythe-in-law. He'd appreciate it if I thought it over as I had done with the condom factory when I was living up among the hippies. He mumbled something like "Jeez, Matty, sometimes you can be a real tightwad, but no offense if it works for you."

With the light falling on his crafty old face I saw the very same little boy who used to snatch away my stuffed rabbit, a memory I can only reconstruct in my imagination from what Mom used to tell me about my earliest years.

I'VE FOUND MYSELF more and more attached to my house. I walk around appreciating every angle of its enveloping floorplan. As the weather improves I can put on a light jacket and go rake up the leaves I left lying last fall on the garden beds. The black soil emerges and soon tiny shoots will be poking up beside what I've cut back. Beyond the fence August Sandstrom has been hammering at the rotten railings of his back deck. Malinda ventures out with me but quickly paws at the study door to be let back in to her cozy bed. I hope she makes it to my seventy-fourth birthday let alone the seventy-fifth.

I have met with my lawyer and have willed to my half-sisters and their offspring full rights to everything. When I told them about it they said they were sure I'll live to ninety-five. At times I believe them, but if it's true I'll have to adopt a third dog. I do plan to stay in this house till my death. I'd rather die here than in a so-called retirement community. The Sandstroms aren't leaving either. They're among the few sets of neighbors that haven't gone off to warmer climates. Ezra started the trend. He was sick of our humid summers and frigid winters. Now he's got dry air and warm sun and hiking and elderly tennis matches and the socializing he so soon missed after moving in with me.

Olive Sandstrom had been on a search for someone to introduce me to and then leave it to the desires of two middle-aged gay men to make something of it. The Sandstroms are deep believers in coupledom, but in my renewed bachelorhood I often feel it as a reproach. Not that they blame me any more than Ezra, but they do lament our lives having grown apart so quickly. "I'm just not much good at making adjustments," I've told them.

This morning Olive knocked on my front door to suggest a dog walk. With Malinda preferring her bed we no longer drive her out to the forest preserve for real runs. About all I can coax her into is a stroll around our long block with its fascinating pee smells from dogs of the newer residents. She needs a good minute at each curbstone, gate post, or bush and is compelled to circle every tree trunk entangling her leash.

Poop bags in my pocket we three set out through the front gate. Olive got reminiscing about meeting August at Northwestern's history department back when she was a young secretary, exactly the professional relationship my mother had found herself in with Henry Blythe a generation earlier. Olive had been just old enough to start worrying she'd be alone for life. I said that was absurd for a young woman of thirty, but I wasn't taking into account that she'd come of age a few years before my flower-power era. "Yet I hadn't begun to worry about being alone before I was almost fifty," I told her. "Oh, you worried," Olive declared, "you simply didn't know it. What do you think all your running around was about?"

She has always interpreted my old sex life as me avoiding the uncertainties of love. I wish I could remember more of our conversation while we dawdled behind Malinda or had to tug her on from behind. I didn't want to argue but I did make the case that I enjoyed living alone. I've always been self-sufficient and like to organize my daily life as neatly as I can. Ezra created a never-ending fount of stuff: kitchen stocked for months ahead, clothes closet jammed, dresser drawers overflowing, toiletries galore, piles of unread magazines and barely skimmed newspapers. It was a relief to see all of that go. "Didn't you partly miss it?" Olive wanted to know. "Not in the least," I said feeling defensive.

I did concede that a trip to Santa Fe wouldn't have been the worst thing for me, but I don't like airplanes, especially these days, and I certainly can't leave Malinda as she is now. When she heard her name the dog promptly took a notion to squat in front of the hideous overbuilt chateau that has filled the lot of a perfectly adequate ranch house where the Whittemores once lived. Poop on grass is harder to collect than poop on cement. I pulled up a clump of lawn that left a bald spot. Olive assured me no one was home to see. Those new people have a condo in the city for the work week and only come up on Friday nights.

I put forth the idea that some of us are not inclined to be coupled. Olive reminded me how delighted I'd been when at last Ezra moved in. "You were an entirely new person," she claimed. "You thanked me a hundred times for bringing you someone to love." Yes, I thought, someone to love, that was it, not necessarily someone to live with but someone I'd do anything for, someone who could always depend on me, someone whose quirks I would generously put up with. It was where I'd failed.

"Is it because your mother left you behind and went off to pursue love among the ruins?" That's how Olive put it after we'd made it around the block with the lagging dog and I'd been invited in for lunch. She caught August up on our talk, one they've been having with me for some time now, but lately they've been getting a whiff of what August calls a change in my atmosphere. He thinks it's the opposite of what I'd been carrying around when they first knew me. "Back then it was a certain hesitance," he said, "but now you seem ready for something new, I don't know what. Well, let's have a jollifying lunch." So I agreed to stay.

I know they only want for me what they have themselves. They can't imagine being without one another so how can I be without a man to settle down with? While they talked of Hilding's spring recital and Kristin's ballet pupils I puzzled over love itself, what it has been for some and not perhaps for me. But surely I learned it from my loving grandmother, and Mom never let me feel unloved. After losing Dad didn't she deserve—I looked down at Malinda asleep by my feet under the lunch table. I remembered how Anthony Garston had talked about yearning for a life free of meaning, a life of only hunger and thirst, digestion and elimination, and the comforts of warmth and touch, Malinda's life, a baby's life, soon an old man's—all of us back where we'd begun. Why burden another person with it? If you're not lucky enough to die at the same time one of you will be left alone anyway. Had Olive ever thought of that? She was the younger of the two as I was by a few years with Ezra. In our brief time together he and I had each forestalled the inevitable by taking our miraculous little pills. We'd been happy in our bed. I hadn't missed different bodies as I'd feared I might. But desire does wane and life-long self-sufficiencies begin to take precedence.

I'd never learned quite how to accommodate other habits and neither, it turned out, had he. How extremely male of each of us!

"See what I meant by your atmosphere, Matt?" August's voice had startled me.

"Oh, I'd been thinking of something else, sorry."

They were proposing a movie night with the Bensons, the only other neighbor couple from the old days. She's on a walker and he's on a cane, and they have helpers coming and going and no more long-haired dachshunds. We could take them a supper and a DVD one night next week, didn't I think? I said it depended on the movie. But they're as sharp-witted as ever despite their legs beginning to fail after their last dachshund died. "But I'd prefer one in color," I told the Sandstroms. Naturally August liked Bergman films because he didn't need to read the subtitles. Now he pulled out his phone and checked Netflix. It took us fifteen minutes of searching through to agree on something Olive felt would be cheerful enough and August didn't judge too stupid so the Bensons wouldn't feel condescended to. I had nothing to suggest after all the exploding car chases Ezra used to have us watch, his idea of a Saturday night. We finally settled on a popular comedy about a tourist hotel in India, quite a stretch from *Pather Panchali*. I still haven't tracked that one down and am no longer inclined to try.

TODAY I FIND myself thinking about my half-sisters. When they were little I used to joke that, put together, they would add up to one whole sister, but then I would only be one quarter-brother to each of them. I imagine I was teaching them fractions. I'm six years older than Margaret and eight older than Henrietta, so we hardly grew up as a trio, but I did serve as their funny fractional older brother who lived at their grandmother's house, so we'd see each other one place or the other.

I see the Heath side more often now because unlike the Blythes they've never left the North Shore. The younger ones must think of me as the reclusive elder cousin in that weird "modern" house, which John Heath II will never get to buy out from under my half-sisters, dammit! Why am I taking stock of them all? When I finally stop going to the office I won't even have colleagues. I must make an effort to visit Henrietta soon. We always have fun talking, and it's not all about her progeny or her Giorgio's retirement hobbies. Henrietta's the one person who doesn't think I should be someone I'm not. Maybe it's because I always sided with her when she was little, throwing her fits or putting on that stubborn glower that used to drive Mom crazy. Margaret was the good girl who followed Pop Henry around like his shadow, but Henrietta would never join in whether down in the Evanston basement with the artifacts or in the faraway ruins of Xanthus. In my files I keep a postcard she sent me from there. It says: "Dear Quarter Brother, can't you rescue me from this sweltering dump? I want to go skating with you on the frozen lagoons. Love from the best half of your sister."

She ended up marrying her dad's Italian grad student, and she's at home in that world now that it's hers. I do love Henrietta. I imagine I would do anything for her. I'm sure she can count on me. There! I feel better. Talking with the Sandstroms last week was more upsetting than I realized. But I do love them too, maybe simply because they're right next door and we depend on each other. We all had a good time with the Bensons despite the silly sentimental movie, but an evening with older couples has a way of making me feel alone. At least Malinda was sleeping by my side on their couch. The aging Bensons made much of her, aware as they are of what's coming some day to each of us.

My own office work steadily goes on, a gigantic continuous, all-consuming math problem without a final answer, an absorbing never-ending series of calculations, plussing and minussing over the years. I don't need to add up all my old clients, involved as I've been in the minutiae of their lives, or all my various colleagues—cheerful comrades or shy hoverers over desks or blank starers into screens. My daytime environment has always been benign, constant, serene if never exactly intimate. The others have known each other better than I've ever known any one of them, and so it remains. I've invited no one out to my house. I've occasionally gone for dinner with a bunch after work and all were more talkative than I. No one has ever probed into my privacies though Ezra was heartily welcomed at holiday parties and summer barbecues in the park. They all know Richie because he's had so many volatile dealings with us, and they like to joke how totally unrelated I seem to my crazy cousin. He has taken the focus off me for which I'm grateful. I get away by regaling the office with Richie Heath stories. They love the lambskin saga, however often I've had to recite it for new employees. "Matthew, tell 'em how you got your start in the money business!"

My work has provided much stability and I'm not yet willing to confirm a retirement date before the looming last quarter of my century. I still cling to a number of long-term clients who say I know them inside out and I probably do. Without them will my life have any useful daily function? Tending my garden and nursing my dog and keeping up with house repairs only affects my half-acre of this planet. But the time will come soon when I'll be saying farewell at some embarrassingly overdone retirement party.

I know one who will actually miss me and that's Evelyn Grandy at the front desk. She's been sitting there almost as long as I've been in my little corner office with its street view. She has countless grandchildren out in her western suburb, but at sixty-six she still comes in determined to work as long as she's able. Yesterday we sat in the lounge on her coffee break or in my case for a second cup of hot tea. We went through the litany of Grandy offspring and heard all the unmemorable details of her large and much loved family. Evelyn is a satisfied woman, and she counts me as one of the people she loves. She says so all too often. Perhaps I did take her especially under my wing when she got the job. Perhaps I've made her feel depended on and appreciated more than the others have. Whatever our bond is, it's happened without me noticing quite how. I don't question it.

Yesterday she said she wished I would never completely retire. "It wouldn't be the same if you weren't here, Matt," she said, "and what's old age anyways, huh?" I told her my life wouldn't be the same without her morning greetings or our confabs in the lounge and her cautioning me not to work too late after hours when she's locking up. I assured her I haven't quite decided when to quit and she said neither has she. She raised five children with her husband, but that never kept her out of work for more than a month of maternity leave. Of course, her mother lived with them in those days, and there was always an aunt or two and several cousins to call in. "The way it used to be," she'll say with a wistful puff out her soft cheeks.

I'm thinking also of my Aunt Alicia back in my own earliest days, her living with Grandmother and Mom, helping out or not being all that much of a help. I remember Mom used to say, "Oh, that Alicia! Our brittle little spats, our tiptoeing around each other back then—there were our husbands off in the war and there were our babies and our mother-in-law and what a nervous time it was for the whole world! And you were peacefully sleeping through it all, Matty, a little oblivious blob of life waiting for what you had no idea of yet. Poor thing!" That sounds like Mom to me.

Evelyn Grandy used to ask thoughtfully after my mother's health and came to the memorial service along with some of my colleagues. She always had something to ask about Ezra, what projects he was working on now, how he'd ever learned to figure out all that stuff about buildings and bridges and overpasses. I had no idea myself. At home he wasn't particularly inclined to fix anything. I was the one who replaced a dripping faucet's gasket or installed a new security lock on a door. But to Evelyn my Ezra was a wonder and she was filled with grief when he moved away. In that, she's another Olive.

No one at the office has ever learned of my viral status. Only Beau and the Sandstroms and Sally and her Samuel know. When I die will it finally come out? Will Henrietta be terribly hurt that I hadn't trusted her enough? But it isn't that. I haven't wanted to worry her. She's got enough going on in her life. Besides I will never know what anyone thinks of me after I'm dead. I will be free of all opinions, of loves and disappointments. I'm not sure it's a welcome thought.

NOW THAT he's flown back home to Colorado I want to hold onto the afternoon I spent with old Beau Templeton. Helen was rushing about seeing family and neighborhood friends, and she thanked me effusively for taking him off her hands for their last day. With his poor eyesight Beau can't go out on his own, so I picked him up in my electric Leaf and we drove silently and smoothly as if floating down a meandering stream to my house for lunch.

I made us club sandwiches, if not quite as tasty as the old Sweet Shop's, and we went to sit outside by the blue pool in the spring air. I'd already turned on the spouting frog. The sun was high enough to fill the courtyard, warming the cushions on the wrought-iron chairs where we sat and ate with Malinda stretched out on the shining flagstones at our feet. We talked about his eyes, about our charitable causes, and about his enforced retirement so I'd have an idea of how I might soon be feeling myself.

Beau suggested I come out and stay awhile in Denver. I could take the train if I didn't want to fly. This time he didn't mention how I could also bus down to New Mexico. He'd given up on me and Ezra years ago. As for going to Colorado I pointed regretfully at my dozing dog, and Beau understood what I meant. So we talked on about our families and how we get tired more easily these days. But Beau has not stopped doing things. He's still committed to his political revolution and says it's Vietnam that started it all for him. He's so full of disgust at the present mess the country's in that the Democratic Socialist in him has to keep on fighting.

"I'm more likely to sit and observe it all in despair," I told him, "not that I've ever done much to help." Beau reminded me that my donations continue to make a difference, but I said it was a minimal sacrifice. "And look at me here by myself in this grand Roman-Japanese villa," I said, "while you and Helen have stayed in that little house where you squeezed yourselves in with three kids!" Then Beau said, "It's simply how you and me, how we've each found our best way to live, Matt. From the start we two have been very different." But then he added, "And yet, old pal, listen, we really do know each other, don't we?" It was all he had to say for me to sense what I was worth to him.

Whatever Denny or Ezra or anyone before or after or in between once told me about us two together has never felt as true as what Beau said in that quiet way. Sure, the others all meant it truly back then and maybe I believed them, but what is it about time, Dr. Mary? I wish I could ask her that now. Am I dodging again? And why can't I let myself truly love a man I've been in bed with? Other men can, can't they? When I'd failed with Ezra Pomfret I was too ashamed to call up Dr. Mary. But last night after I'd driven Beau back to his brother-in-law's I tried to locate her online. Of all the Colemans out there I couldn't identify mine. Perhaps she'd been older than I thought. Perhaps she'd taken a new husband's name. I'd like to imagine her having retreated up into the Vermont mountains I used to pretend she'd come down from. That's what I'll tell myself.

Beau and I have been friends since our first year of life even if we can't remember how it started. I lost my father early in our sandbox days. Beau lost his mother the summer after high school. I know I'd been a comfort. He certainly comforted me when I most needed it. He could simply have written a letter, but instead he flew all the way back here to tell me I'd be all right. Ever since, in letters and visits, in our not very intense or emotional way, we have been able to tell each other about our lives. We have kept in touch. That's what we said after I drove him back to Helen's brother's house: "Keep in touch, Matt." "You too, Beau." That kind of touch isn't physical but it has the effect of it. I think of all the men's bodies I've once or dozens of times touched all over but never Beau's beyond a fully-clothed hug or two. I've never thought of touching him any other way or wanted to. It would be unnecessary.

And yet earlier after we'd driven out to the forest preserve for a walk in the mild April breeze, having left sleepy Malinda in her corner, and we were walking across the softening earth on the not-yet-mown yellowed grass that slopes down to the edge of one of the lagoons, Beau had to take my hand because in the low sunlight he couldn't quite be sure of his footing. So we two old men carefully made our way, hand-in-hand, downhill toward the opaquely glowing water where some dozen mallard ducks paddled about and the returning songbirds chirped at each other from the budding trees. We stood there side by side and listened and looked off into the reddening sky to the west. I want to leave myself in that moment of us standing together, of me and my oldest friend, as if for the last time.